THE UPPER HAND

DC O'Connell Crime Thriller Series
Book 1

By
A L Fraine

The book is Copyright © to Creative Edge Studios Ltd, 2019.
No part of this book may be reproduced without prior permission of the copyright holder.

All locations, events, and characters within this book are either fictitious, or have been fictionalised for the purposes of this book.

Book List

DC O'Connell British Crime Thrillers
First Hand – Prequel
The Upper Hand – Book 1
Idle Hands – Book 2
Out of Hand – Book 3

Acknowledgements

Thank you to my wife and family for all your support and for believing in me. Love you all.

Thank you to my proof readers for your help.

Thank you to Hanna Elizabeth, my Editor, for her hard work.

Thank you to Barry Hutchison, for being a great sounding board in this process.

Thank you to Surrey Police for their time and help.

Thank you to my readers, because without you, none of this would be possible.

Enjoy.

Note:
This book is written in British English.

Table of Contents

Book List 2
Acknowledgements 3
Table of Contents 4
CHAPTER 1 5
CHAPTER 2 14
CHAPTER 3 19
CHAPTER 4 32
CHAPTER 5 43
CHAPTER 6 49
CHAPTER 7 59
CHAPTER 8 79
CHAPTER 9 82
CHAPTER 10 97
CHAPTER 11 104
CHAPTER 12 112
CHAPTER 13 122
CHAPTER 14 127
CHAPTER 15 137
CHAPTER 16 139
CHAPTER 17 147
CHAPTER 18 156
CHAPTER 19 161
CHAPTER 20 171
CHAPTER 21 184
CHAPTER 22 186
CHAPTER 23 197
CHAPTER 24 207
CHAPTER 25 223
CHAPTER 26 235
CHAPTER 27 250
CHAPTER 28 256
CHAPTER 29 258
Author Note 261
Book List 262

CHAPTER 1

Three Weeks ago.

"Hey man, thanks for the night out, I really appreciate it," Mark said, offering his hand to his friend, who took it with a firm grip.

"Not a problem, it was good to catch up, you know?"

"Yeah, it was," Mark replied with a half-hearted smile.

"Look, don't feel bad. You don't owe me anything, alright? This was my treat. We all have money troubles from time to time. It's no big deal. You'll get through this. I know you will."

Mark nodded and tried to give a better, more enthusiastic smile. He wasn't sure it worked. "I hope so."

"If you need anything, just ask, alright? I'll see what I can do for you."

"How about a loan?"

Adrian smiled. "I'd love to man, I would, honestly..."

"I know mate. I'm kidding. Thanks for the drinks, though. We should do it again sometime."

"Defo. Let me know some dates that work for you, and I'll run it by the missus."

Mark gave his friend's hand one more shake before he let go. "I will. Catch you later."

"Take care of yourself," Adrian answered, and with a final nod and wave, started off down the road.

Mark watched him go for a second before turning the other direction and making his way north, away from Guildford Town Centre towards the estates beyond the A3.

He'd only had a couple of drinks with some snacks, and could barely feel any effects from the alcohol at all. But then, that wasn't surprising. Beer had become a close friend of his since the bankruptcy.

He'd not seen Adrian in years, but then out of nowhere, he'd got in touch over Facebook of all places. Mark guessed he'd accepted a friend request at some point, although he couldn't remember it.

Adrian had been an old school friend, and it had been great to see him and find out what he'd been up to. He'd known a little about Mark's own misfortune, which was the reason he'd reached out, or at least, that's what Adrian had said.

Mark hadn't gone into all the details about what he'd done. There was no need for that. Few people knew everything. Not even his wife knew about the drug-fuelled nights at hotels with a couple of working girls.

You bloody idiot, he thought, thinking back to the way he'd ruined everything. Taking over his dad's business had been amazing. Suddenly he'd had money. Lots of money. But he didn't know how to run a business, and after his dad had stepped away from it, it soon took a dive.

Things just got steadily worse as he took to drink, drugs, and just throwing the money away.

Now his family didn't want to see him, and his wife... Well, she wasn't exactly the most sympathetic of people.

He soon reached the footbridge that crossed over the A3 and walked up the switchback ascent to the main span that crossed the road below. The streets were fairly quiet, and just one other figure followed him up the bridge.

Mark crossed the highway and walked off into the residential estates on the other side, making a left and right, and then a little further up, walked along a cut-through between roads.

A glance behind him revealed the same man he'd seen on the bridge, still a short distance back, keeping pace with him. Mark frowned, but kept going. It wasn't that far to his home now. The man probably lived on an adjacent street or something.

The thought of returning to the house and seeing his wife produced a feeling of dread in his stomach. He hoped Lisa was asleep. He couldn't be doing with her tonight. He was willing to bet she'd been on the cheap wine again like she did most nights recently, and he'd likely get an earful from her the moment he stepped into the house.

Ugh, that bloody house. He hated it. It was so much smaller than the one they'd had, and on a shitty street with idiot kids who really should be at school and not riding about causing trouble.

It was all they could afford to rent, though, until he got a better job—a subject that was one of Lisa's favourite topics. She seemed to hate him these days. She was always finding something to have a go at him about. His job. Money. The house. The bills. It didn't seem to matter. Everything was his fault.

But then, he couldn't really argue with that. It was his fault. He was the one who spent all the money. He was the one who'd drunk too much, got hooked on smack, and had the occasional orgy with expensive hookers.

Jeez, those had been some fun nights.

Nights he'd never have again unless something changed.

But he couldn't see any light at the end of the tunnel. He couldn't see much reason for hope. Not right now.

His friend, Adrian, reaching out and taking him for a drink had been the first real fun he'd had since everything had gone wrong. It had been fun to reminisce about their days at school and talk about old school friends. He wondered what some of those guys were up to now.

After another left turn, he looked back to see the same man still following him. Mark furrowed his brow as a chill shot up his spine. This seemed odd. Was this guy purposefully following him?

What was he playing at?

He shook his head. *Get a grip, man, what are you thinking?* Why would someone do this?

Mark ploughed on, and as he thought about walking in and getting yelled at by Lisa, he chose to take a longer route with a bit of a loop. That way he could delay getting back home and also see if this guy was really following him. Mark took a right and kept going.

At the end of the street, he turned left and glanced back, spotting the man still following on behind him.

As he got out of sight, around the corner, part of him wanted to run. He wanted to sprint up the road to the next corner and try to lose him.

This was beginning to get a little freaky, and the worries of getting home to an irate Lisa began to fade away, only to be replaced with a growing, gnawing fear that he might be attacked by the man behind him.

Mark quickened his pace, walking as fast as he could. His legs pumped away beneath him, carrying him along the pavement towards the next left where he'd be doubling back on himself, and as he reached the turn, he looked back.

The previous corner wasn't that far back, and Mark paused for a moment on seeing no one there. No one behind him.

Had the man turned away? Maybe he'd gone into a house he'd passed, and the fear he'd been feeling was totally unjustified.

The man rounded the corner.

Mark's stomach fell, and he pressed on, starting up the next street.

He was certain of it now. The man was stalking him. There was no other explanation for it. No one would take the same route he'd just taken. No one. Mark crossed the street as he weighed up his options, taking the opportunity to look back as he checked the road for cars. The man was there again, on the same street, striding up after him.

Shit, shit, shit.

He wanted to run. He desperately wanted to run. It was a deep, guttural instinct that was shouting at him from somewhere deep inside. That man was a threat and the most obvious, and the easiest, thing to do was to break into a sprint and get the hell out of there.

But a small part of him wouldn't let him do it. There was still a nagging doubt that this might still be all in his head, and the man wasn't interested in him. Plus, he wasn't a wimp. He was a grown man, not some child letting his imagination run away with him just because it was late at night and dark.

Thinking about the route ahead, he only had a couple more streets before he was home, but a small voice from somewhere in the back of his mind told him to be careful. *Don't show the man where you live*, he thought.

Between here and his road, Mark remembered a public bench on a corner of the street, and an idea occurred to him.

He'd confront him. If the man really was following him, then maybe Mark should pull himself together and ask the man what the hell he was doing.

He had to admit, the thought of turning around and waiting for the man who'd been shadowing him filled him with what felt like an unreasonable amount of terror, but he did not want to lead him to his house.

Mark reached the end of the road and glanced back again. The man was still there, still striding up the road, his shoulders hunched, his head down, just a dark shadow on the streets.

Mark continued on, turning right, he spotted the bench and made straight for it. He reached it without issue, and sat, looking back up the street from the direction he'd come, waiting for the man to appear.

He felt tense as he waited. His lips pressed tightly together while his right leg bounced nervously. He glanced down at it accusingly, hating that it was giving away his nervousness.

Since when had he become so worried about confrontation? Before all this crap with the business, he'd been the confident one. He'd once thought nothing of going on the offensive in a meeting to try and get what he wanted. Going even further back to his time at school. In hindsight, he'd known for a while that he'd been a bit of a dick.

Had he been a bully? He wasn't sure about that. That sounded like a fairly serious word for his actions back then. Actions he wasn't too proud of.

Mark put his hand on his leg and forced it to stop bouncing as he glanced back up the road.

The man should have appeared by now. Where was he?

As the seconds passed, doubt began to gnaw at the back of his mind. Maybe he'd been an idiot. Maybe the man hadn't been following him.

As the seconds turned into minutes, Mark's need to know where the man was, only deepened. After a few more moments, he stood up and walked back the way he'd come, towards the previous road to have a look. As he approached the corner, he turned in a full circle, checking all around him, but Mark couldn't see the man anywhere.

Taking a deep breath, he stoked his remaining courage as he approached that last corner and looked down the road where he'd last seen the man. But he wasn't there.

The street was empty. No people, no moving cars, nothing.

Strange.

But then, maybe not. Maybe he'd disappeared into one of these houses.

Taking a step back, Mark shrugged. *Strange, but not inexplicable*, he thought.

"Mark Summers," said a voice behind him.

Mark turned. The man was right there. Right in front of him, his face in shadow. The man's arm moved and he felt something being jabbed into his stomach.

A sudden, gut-wrenching pain flooded his body from whatever it was that had been pressed into him. There was a buzzing noise that did not sound at all friendly as his body convulsed and locked up. He fell to the ground with a thud, unable to stop himself in any way, and slammed his head into the pavement. The buzzing stopped, but the excruciating pain did not as Mark tried to pull in a breath.

His vision swam. He had trouble focusing, but he did see the man hold up something dark and blocky. Bright blue-coloured light flared at one end of the device as it buzzed again.

A taser?

"Now who has the upper hand, hmm?" the man said as he made the taser spark a couple more times before he put it away.

Mark grunted and tried to move, but his body still wouldn't listen to him as he watched the man pull something else out of his other pocket and hold it aloft. It was long and thin, and it glinted in the streetlight. The man pressed something on the bottom of it, and liquid squirted out of the tip.

"Time to go night-night," the man said, crouching down beside him and stabbing the syringe into his upper arm. Within moments, darkness claimed him.

CHAPTER 2

Today

"Come on then, down you get," Deborah said to the golden retriever in the back of her car. The dog stood up and hopped out onto the dirt before she closed the boot and locked the vehicle with a press of a button on her key fob. The lights on the car flashed as the bolts slammed home with a satisfying clunk.

Turning towards the track that led into the woods, Deborah saw that Sandy had already made it over there, and stood waiting, wagging her tail in anticipation of the walk ahead and all the wonderful smells she was about to experience.

Deborah smiled and followed, walking onto the track and urging Sandy to go explore. "Off you go, go on," she said.

She started off at a good stride, walking with purpose as she considered her route through the doggy paradise ahead. There were several ways she could go. These tracks all linked up and crisscrossed over each other, meaning she could almost walk a new route every day. Some days, when she had less going on, she'd walk for miles, taking a long, winding journey through the forest, letting Sandy roam far and wide through the foliage. On her busier days, she'd take a shorter route, but she always made time to take Sandy out. She felt it was important that Sandy had some kind of walk every day. Dogs needed that freedom, they needed the exercise.

It didn't feel right to Deborah for Sandy to be stuck in the house or garden all day.

She smiled and said hi to another walker who'd gotten here before her, but there weren't many who came out here this early in the morning. She often had much of the place to herself, but she didn't mind. It gave her time to think about the day and what she was going to do.

Mick had already gone to work, off to the station to catch the train up into London.

She'd decided a long time ago that she might as well get up when he did and head out at roughly the same time. She was up anyway, so why not? She'd thrown on the same clothes as yesterday, scraped her hair back into a ponytail, pulled on her Dubarry boots, and driven their second car out here just like she did every day.

Keeping her pace brisk, she was keen to build up some kind of sweat to warm herself against the fresh morning air and get a bit of exercise in. She felt like she'd put on a little weight recently and was keen to shed it, so she used these walks as a way to get herself moving and push herself.

Sandy seemed to prefer it when she walked quicker anyway. She was always running off ahead and charging through the bushes, just as she was now, ranging wide between the trees and over the leaves on the ground.

Deborah kept going and thought about what they'd be eating tonight as she looked back to try and spot Sandy. She was through the trees, a short distance off the track.

"Sandy," she called out. "Come on, Sandy." But the dog didn't move.

She seemed to have found something, a dead animal maybe? Deborah stopped and called out again, but Sandy just ignored her.

"Sandy! Come here," Deborah ordered. Sandy's head popped up, but she just barked at her before going back to whatever she was chewing on.

"Sandy? Have I got to come in there after you?"

The dog barked again.

"Ugh," she grunted and stepped off the track, walking into the trees and through the low grass. Sandy was next to a tree in a small clearing, but Deborah couldn't see what she was biting, on the other side of it.

It was a large oak with a wide trunk and a thick canopy, and as she stepped out into the small clearing, she noticed that several sticks had been stabbed into the ground around its base in a rough circle.

She didn't pay them much mind though. There were plenty of places throughout the woods where kids had piled sticks up against fallen logs or up against trees to make shelters. Maybe it was some local scout group who'd been up here on an outing.

She rounded the tree to get a better look at what Sandy was gnawing on.

"What have you got there?" she asked, only to freeze in place as she realised that what she'd thought was just another branch sticking out of the tree, was anything but.

From behind the tree, a human arm stuck out at around head height, strung up to the branch above by rope. The hand hung limp, and the skin was an odd pallor.

Deborah's hand shot to her mouth as she gasped. Her heart suddenly began pounding in her chest as a sinking feeling settled into her gut. With the sudden intake of breath, she got her first good whiff of an acrid, metallic stench that went right to the back of her nose, and stayed there.

Her stomach did a summersault.

"Oh, shit," she muttered under her breath. "Sandy. Sandy come here!" she called out, but the dog wouldn't move.

"Goddammit, Sandy," she yelled, and the dog lifted its head to look at her. The fur around Sandy's mouth was stained a deep red.

"Oh god," Deborah muttered as the dog went back to whatever it was gnawing on.

There was nothing for it, she'd have to go get her and see what was on the other side of that trunk. Deborah took a deep breath and immediately regretted it as the smell filled her lungs. She squeezed her hands into fists as she tried to push the fear away. Marching forward, keeping her eyes firmly fixed upon her dog, she reached in to grab her collar, knowing that whatever was strung up against the tree was right above her. She pulled Sandy back to reveal a partially chewed human foot attached to a leg.

Deborah stepped back, pulling Sandy with her, and despite every nerve in her body telling her not to, she looked up.

"Oh crap," she whispered as her stomach heaved and she threw up onto the ground.

CHAPTER 3

Taking another spoonful of muesli, Kate watched local news on the breakfast program with one eye on the clock. She was early, but this was her first day, and she wanted to make sure she got to work with time to spare.

She was keen to get off on the right foot, and first impressions were important. She'd worked hard to get here, and she didn't want to mess it up before she even got started.

Chewing on a new mouthful of her cereal, the news anchor moved on to her second story of the broadcast.

"The parents of missing local man, Mark Summers, gave a press conference today, offering a reward for any information that leads to the discovery of their son. Mark has been missing for three weeks since disappearing in Guildford after a night out. If you have any information on Mark's location, the number to call is on the bottom of the screen."

Surrey might be home to some very wealthy individuals, but like anywhere in the UK, it had its fair share of problems and dangerous people.

Finishing her breakfast with a final spoonful, she placed her bowl in the sink in the kitchenette, grabbed her jacket from the back of a chair and slipped it on, before moving to the nearby mirror to check herself over one last time.

She'd bought a new suit for today, as well as polished her shoes to try to help with that good early impression. She double-checked she had her warrant card, cuffs, money, and phone before she cast a critical eye to her hair.

Reaching up, she pulled her auburn hair back off her shoulders and into a ponytail to keep it out the way. Kate didn't usually wear much makeup, but with this being her first day on a new team, she couldn't resist using just a little bit.

She felt sure that wouldn't last.

Taking a last look in the mirror, her eyes drifted to the shelf on her right, and the photo of her aunt, Fiona. Kate smiled to herself, then flashes of the nightmare that had woken her up last night appeared in her mind, reminding her of events ten years ago. Events she would rather forget.

She reached up and touched the glass in the picture frame. "Well, I made it, Fi. I'm on the Murder Team. Finally. I won't let you down."

Across the room, behind her, the folder that held the letters stood in the bookcase. Its presence weighed heavily on her mind as she looked fondly upon the image of her aunt. She might be gone, but Kate would never forget her aunt and the influence she had on her life.

Turning away, she sucked in a deep breath and let it go, trying to calm the butterflies in her stomach before grabbing her keys and leaving her flat behind.

The drive from her home in north Leatherhead over to the new station in Horsley didn't take long. It was still early, and although the traffic was already beginning to build, there were no holdups along the way.

She was only maybe a minute or so from the building when she heard the familiar sirens of a patrol car approaching from behind. She pulled over to let the vehicle pass, its blue lights flashing as it zipped by at speed.

Kate smiled to herself. She'd done three years as a uniformed officer in several roles and had been in her fair share of Incident Response Vehicles over the years, blasting through traffic with the siren and lights going. Nothing got the blood and adrenaline pumping like racing to a scene in a patrol car at high speed.

But it was the investigation side of things that had always appealed to her, and she'd known that ultimately, she wanted to be a detective. She achieved that goal a year ago, working on various cases until she was finally eligible to be transferred to the specialised Murder Team

Moments later she rounded the corner into Horsley on the main road that snaked through the quiet Surrey village. The station came into view from behind some trees as she navigated the S-bend.

Rounding the second corner, she pulled off the road and into the small public car park out front and found a suitable empty spot, making sure not to park in any of the reserved spaces for the officers further up the chain of command.

That would not be a good way to start the day.

She knew there was another, private car park out back for them to use, but given this was her first day and she thought it better to stay here.

Turning off the car, she took another few calming breaths and checked the time. She was over half an hour early for her shift, but now that she was here, she couldn't help feeling nervous. She'd been here before on and off while in uniform and during her first year as a detective, always eyeing it, and the officers who worked here, with envy.

That's where she wanted to be, she'd thought. She wanted to be on the Murder Team, tracking down the worst of the worst. The real dregs of society.

Well Kate, she thought, *you've made it. You're here. Now get a grip, go in there, and make a good first impression.*

Making sure her ID was in place; she stepped out of her car and approached the looming building. Its three storeys rose up above her, looking somehow more intimidating now, than they had ever done on her previous visits. But she ploughed on, pushing those nerves away and walked in the front door, into the reception, and up to the main desk.

A woman in uniform smiled at her as she approached.

"Morning," the Station Officer said in greeting.

"Hi. I'm DC Kate O'Connell? I'm joining the Murder Team today."

"Aaah yes, we're expecting you. Welcome. You're in early."

Kate smiled. "Just want to make a good impression."

"Of course. Well, sign in. You'll have to take a seat, DCI Dean isn't in yet. But I doubt he'll be long."

"Okay, thanks," Kate answered as she signed the book and stepped away from the reception desk. She noticed the chairs up against the far wall, along with the other two people sat in here waiting, neither of which looked like police officers to her, and decided to keep her distance. Besides, she wanted to be on her feet anyway. She had too much nervous energy to sit and relax.

There were the usual notice boards with all kinds of posters and information pinned to them, none of which really interested her. But nearby, she spotted a series of framed photos that depicted the building being built and then renovated.

Kate knew a little of the history of the place already. It was a newly-built site, planned initially as a commercial building where businesses could rent out space, but the developer went under so it sat unfinished for a while until a local man, a self-made billionaire, bought it and donated it to the police.

The philanthropist wanted to help make a safer county with better policing, and this was just one of the ways he was helping to do that.

Kate passed the time admiring the photos and reading the descriptions below them that detailed the history of the building. Some of the images showed it being built and then renovated, as well as pictures of the opening ceremony with the billionaire and the local Mayor. The notes below each image filled in some of the blanks in her knowledge.

"DC O'Connell?" said a male voice from behind her. Kate turned and smiled at the man she found approaching her from the reception desk.

"Good morning, DCI Dean," Kate answered, recognising him right away. He was a stocky man in his mid-forties with a balding head that he kept shaved. She'd met him several times before in the line of duty, and again during her application to join the Surrey Murder Team.

"You're eager to get started then?" he asked.

"Of course, and thank you for having me, sir. I really appreciate it."

"Glad to have you. Come on, follow me, let's head upstairs. We can have a quick chat in my office."

"Very good, sir," she answered, and followed him through the station. Eventually, they reached a room on the side of the Murder Team's office and he led her inside, offering her a seat in front of his desk. DCI Dean removed his jacket and took his place opposite her with a sigh.

"So, you found the place okay?"

"Yes, sir. It's a difficult building to miss," she answered.

He nodded. "Yeah, it's not subtle. So, welcome to the team. I read through your file again the other day. You've got an impressive record, O'Connell. I think you'll be an asset to the team."

"Thank you, sir. I'll certainly try to live up to your expectations."

"I'm sure you will. So, did you always want to be a detective?

"I have for a while, yes, sir. My dad served for many years, so that probably influenced me a bit."

"I saw that. He was part of the RUC in Northern Ireland during the troubles, right?"

Kate nodded. She didn't know a lot about that period of her father's life. He didn't like to talk about it, so she usually avoided the subject. She knew he'd served in the Royal Ulster Constabulary, she also knew that it was during this time that he'd met her mother, who was an Irish native, unlike her father who was British by birth. "Only towards the end, but yes. My parents left Ireland and moved to the UK before I was born."

"Well, we're pleased to have you with us, DC O'Connell. Now, I'm going to provisionally assign you to one of the team. I want to see how you get on before I decide where best to have you," the DCI said, rising from his chair.I "If you'd like to follow me?"

Kate got up and followed DCI Dean through the office, feeling the eyes of the room on her, watching the new girl.

"Hey, Nathan," one of them called out. "Looks like you've got a new Scully."

With a raised eyebrow she glanced at the man who'd spoken, wondering what that was all about. The short man smiled to himself as he turned and nodded to her in greeting. "Mornin'," he said.

"That's enough of your smart mouth, DS Taylor," the DCI said.

"Skipper," the Detective Sergeant answered with a nod of deference as Kate followed the DCI across the room.

"Ignore them," the DCI said over his shoulder with a note of exasperation in his voice.

Kate let a slight smile play over her face. "Don't worry, I can give as good as I get."

The DCI returned her grin. "Good, glad to hear it. Okay, here we are. DC Katherine O'Connell, meet DS Nathan Halliwell." Kate grimaced at the sound of her full name. "You'll be partners while you learn the ropes, Kate. Okay, Nathan?"

"Of course, Skipper," Nathan replied, sitting back in his chair. His eyes flicked between the DCI and herself.

She smiled at him and offered her hand. "Nice to meet you."

Nathan glanced at her hand for a moment before reaching out and giving it a cursory shake that was anything but firm. "And you," he replied, looking her in the eye with an expression that gave her the impression he was assessing her somehow.

To Kate he looked a little scruffy, with messy, mousy-brown hair that looked like it could do with a cut and an old suit that might not have seen an iron for weeks. The top two buttons on his shirt were open, and he didn't wear a tie either.

"Well, as much as I hate to leave this scintillating conversation, I have a lot to do today, so I'll leave you to settle in. That'll be your desk, Kate," the DCI said, indicating the empty one behind Nathan. "I'll check in on you later, I'm sure Nathan will find you something to do."

"Thank you, sir," Kate replied happily.

The DCI nodded to her and then turned to Nathan. "Don't you scare her off, alright? We're short staffed as it is."

Kate noticed Nathan roll his eyes at the comment and look away. She looked back at the DCI who winked at her and then walked off. Kate watched him go and then looked back at her new partner.

"So, Nathan, how's things? Are you busy?"

"I guess," he replied, and she got the feeling he didn't really want to talk to her. But given they were going to be partners, at least for a little while, she wouldn't be put off by him that easily.

She walked over to her desk and sat in the chair, testing out its movement and adjusting the height of the seat to suit her.

Satisfied, she looked back over to Nathan. He was turned mostly away from her, looking through something on his desk.

"Well, I'm looking forward to working with you," she said.

"That'll make a nice change," he replied.

"Have you been on the Murder Team long?"

"Yep," he said.

She considered leaving it there, as he really didn't seem to want to talk, but after a moment she decided to push a little further. "How long, if you don't mind me asking?"

Nathan lifted his head and turned to look at her. He looked her up and down with a frown on his face. "Long enough."

Kate shrugged, deciding to leave that line of questioning and try another tack. "What are you working on?"

Nathan raised an eyebrow at her, apparently a little surprised by her tenacity. He sat back and placed the end of his pen in his mouth. "Just some theories."

"Anything I should know?" she continued. She wasn't going to let him off the hook that easily. She had wondered if he might ask any questions back, but so far, nothing.

"Not if you like your reputation," he replied, his eyebrows raised.

"Oh," Kate answered, not quite sure what he meant by that.

"Get yourself settled in. I'll find something for you to do in a minute," he said, turning back to his desk. Kate watched him look away, not too sure what to make of him, and then looked over the office, noticing the eyes of a couple of the other officers on her. Most of them looked away as she met their gaze.

She looked back at Nathan and noted the position of their desks as they related to the others. They were slightly apart and on their own. She wondered if there might be some significance to this, as she turned to face her desk. A note stuck to the edge of her keyboard had her temporary login details written on it, but otherwise the desk was clean and clear.

She checked through the drawers, and in the bottom one—a deep filing drawer—something vaguely round and shiny glinted in the shadows. She eyed it curiously and then reached in and fished it out.

Turning the strange creation over in her hands, she suddenly realised it was a tin foil hat. She looked at it in confusion for a moment and heard a stifled laugh a short distance away in the office. She looked up to see the detective who had made the Scully comment watching her. He smirked again.

Kate sighed but couldn't help the smile that played over her face. With a shrug, she placed the hat on her head, looked over to DS Taylor and struck a pose for him with her hand on her hip.

"Am I interrupting something?"

Kate looked up to see the DCI stood nearby, this time with another officer just behind him.

Kate reached up and removed the hat. "Just giving as good as I get, sir."

A slight smile played over DCI Dean's face. "Glad to hear it," he said, and then glanced over to DS Taylor, who quickly busied himself at his desk.

"What's up, Skip?" Nathan asked.

"I've just taken a call from Duty Officer Dyson who's on the scene of a murder, and I'm going to assign it to you, Nathan."

"Me, sir?" Nathan asked, sounding surprised.

"I'll be your SIO, but with Kate here, I think you two can take this one on between you."

"Are you sure?" Nathan sounded cautious.

"Nathan," the DCI sighed, "you know what you're doing. It's been a long time since the Steed case, and you've proven yourself many times since. I have full confidence in you. Plus, this sounds like your kind of case."

"My kind of case?"

Kate caught a look of exasperation from the officer behind DCI Dean, who did not look impressed with this conversation.

"Sounds ritualistic from what Dyson said on the phone. Anyway, like I said, I'll be your SIO, and I'll probably have Mason here be Deputy SIO and liaise between us, but this'll be your case, Nathan. Understood?"

"Of course, Skipper."

"I'm heading there now, the details are on the system, follow us there."

"Thank you, sir," Nathan said.

The DCI looked over at Kate and smiled. "Looks like you're jumping in the deep end Miss O'Connell. We'll see if you sink or swim."

Kate gave him a curt nod. "I'm a good swimmer, sir."

He smirked at her answer as he turned and walked towards the exit.

Kate cringed. *Good swimmer? Idiot*, she admonished herself. Beside her, Nathan checked his computer.

He read a short briefing, made a few quick notes, stood up, and pulled his jacket on. "Right, we've got a murder scene to attend."

"Let's go," she said, grabbing the tin foil hat off her desk and screwing it up into a ball as she walked. Taking aim, Kate threw it over the intervening desks where it caught DS Taylor on the face and landed in his lap as he jumped in shock.

DS Taylor looked up at her in surprised indignation. Kate shrugged, and with a smile, turned to follow Nathan who was giving her an appraising look.

"Everything okay?" she asked.

"Yeah, I think so… Come on, let's hit the road."

CHAPTER 4

Nathan led her outside and into the car park, making for a nearby unmarked vehicle.

"What've we got?" Kate asked.

"We'll talk on the way, get in," Nathan answered her and climbed into the driver's seat. Kate settled herself into the passenger side as Nathan pulled out into traffic.

"So?" Kate asked once they were a little way down the road.

"A body's been found in the Ranmore woods just south of here."

Kate nodded and swallowed as a couple of butterflies appeared in her stomach. The little bit of fun and banter in the office was over now, it was time to get to work and show the skipper what she could do. "Nothing like getting stuck right in on the first day," she said, noticing a slight wobble in her voice, which she knew was just first day nerves.

"Everything okay?" he asked.

"Of course."

Nathan nodded. "Good," he replied, sounding entirely unconvinced.

"Look, I know what I'm doing. I'm a hard worker, and I won't let you down. I'm in this for the long haul."

Nathan glanced at her, pressing his lips together in what looked like consternation. "Admirable. But you'll be moved on soon enough."

"Moved on?"

"To someone else on the team. Look, don't worry about it. This always happens, it's not a big deal," Nathan explained.

"Is this something to do with the Scully comment, and the tin hat?"

Nathan didn't answer for a moment as he concentrated on the road ahead. Eventually, he replied. "Let's just concentrate on the case, shall we?"

Kate nodded, but with a look of confusion on her face. "Sure, why not?" she answered, but was curious to know more.

The rest of the short drive passed in relative silence until Nathan pulled the vehicle off towards the entrance of a muddy car park off a country road. It was guarded by a patrol car and a uniformed officer who waved them to a stop.

Kate pulled out her warrant card and showed it to the officer while Nathan did the same. They were waved through, and Nathan parked up a little way into the open area. There was already a range of emergency vehicles parked up in here and tape cordoning the area off. Kate climbed out of the car and met Nathan on the other side as a uniformed officer walked over.

"Can I help?"

Nathan showed the officer his card. Kate did the same. "DC's Halliwell and O'Connell from the Murder Team, we've been assign-"

"Nathan! Well, I should have expected you," said a sergeant who followed the first officer over. "Thanks, I'll take them in," the sergeant said to the constable who'd greeted them.

"Sergeant Dyson," Nathan greeted the tall man with carefully styled dark hair.

"Should be right up your alley, this one," Dyson commented.

"Is that right?" Nathan replied, his voice sceptical.

"Well, I've not seen one like this before, let's put it that way," Dyson explained, and then looked over at Kate. "Another new partner?"

"DC O'Connell," she said, offering her hand.

"Well, you *are* in for a treat. Come on, it's this way. DCI Dean's already here."

Kate frowned at his 'treat' comment as the sergeant led them out of the car park and along a muddy pathway into the surrounding woodland, passing the occasional officer along the way. She noted a few boot prints in the mud along the path that had been marked for further investigation.

"So what can you tell us so far?" Nathan asked.

"The body was found this morning by a dog walker. Her dog ran into the trees and wouldn't come out. She went to get it and that's when she found the body."

"Is she still here?"

"The walker? Yeah, she's back in the car park if you want to speak with her. We've taken a statement. She called the police right away, but I think she might need some counselling after what she saw."

"It's bad?"

"Messed up, mate. Messed. Up. Anyway, we think we know who the victim is, we've got his clothes and a photo ID on-site. Okay, here we are, through here."

Kate followed on behind Nathan and Sergeant Dyson who led the way through the trees, over the uneven ground covered in dead leaves. She could already smell that acrid stench that hung around the dead as they slowly decomposed. She'd encountered it several times, and it was always quite distinct and vomit-inducing.

Interestingly, she'd seen more dead bodies and horrific injuries in uniform than as a CID officer, which was apparently typical as it was the uniforms that always attended RTC's and secured the scenes of murders.

Ahead, Kate could see a large tree that was surrounded by police tape. Officers stood around, guarding the area or going about their assigned tasks, including DCI Dean, DI Mason, and a Scene of Crime Officer in white coveralls who was examining something out of view behind the large oak. Reaching the clearing that surrounded the tree, Kate noticed the branches that had been stuck into the mud in a circle around the trunk and paused for a moment as her mind went back to when she was sixteen and a particular report she'd read.

She shook her head and dismissed it. They were not the same thing, not really.

She walked around the crime scene, each step around the trunk bringing more of the horror into view until they stood just behind DCI Dean.

A man she did not recognise had been strung up against the mighty oak. Ropes wrapped around his wrists and torso were tied to the branches, keeping the man upright in a Christ-like pose, as if he'd been crucified.

His pasty white skin was covered in deep cuts all over his naked body as if the killer had been writing something on him. He was covered in dried blood that had run onto the ground, and into some kind of white powder that had been poured out in circles around the tree.

"I mean, have you ever seen anything like this?" Sergeant Dyson asked Nathan, his voice a low whisper, betraying how uncomfortable the scene made him feel. "Because I haven't."

Nathan just stared at the corpse, an intense frown on his face as he studied the scene.

Kate had seen death. She'd seen murder victims and casualties of car accidents, and it was never pretty. Death, and murder especially, was ugly. There was always a sense of loss. Of a life being wasted. But the death she'd seen so far was nothing like this.

This was not a crime of passion or a violent assault. This was careful, methodical, and planned. The killer took his time over this, possibly even enjoying his work.

The gory nature of the scene didn't bother her so much. She'd seen injuries of all kinds, many of them much worse than this, but it was what the scene suggested about what had happened here that hit home. Still, Kate felt sure she'd be able to remain detached from it, but her brain had other ideas.

Again, Kate's mind went right back to when she was sixteen, and the reports she'd read about her Aunt's murder. For a brief moment, Kate felt sick to her stomach. She turned and reached for a nearby tree for support as she leaned over and took a few deep, cleansing breaths to steady her nerves.

For a moment, all she could think about was getting control of her body, so she concentrated on her breathing, pulling the air in and then blowing it out in long, slow, steady breaths, doing her best to ignore the smell of the cadaver. After a few seconds, the feeling of dizziness began to fade and she started to feel better, if a little embarrassed.

She shook her head as she stood up straight again. She knew it wasn't the body. She'd seen bodies before. She could handle that, it was everything else that went along with it that reminded her of how her Aunt died, and what Kate had done as a teenager.

But she pushed all that back and shut it away. She needed to compartmentalise this. This was not her aunt and a totally different situation.

Feeling better, she turned and stepped up beside Nathan, who was giving her a curious look.

"Everything okay?" he whispered.

"I'm fine, don't worry," she replied, looking up to make sure the DCI hadn't seen her wobble. It didn't look like he had.

Nathan nodded slowly, a look of curiosity on his face.

DCI Dean turned to face them having finished a brief chat between him, DI Mason, and the SOCO officer. "Alright, I've seen what I need to. It's all yours, Nathan. Let me know what you need, and I'll make sure you have it. You have my full support and confidence." Behind him, DI Mason rolled his eyes. "I'll see you back at the station, I have other cases to deal with today."

"Understood," Nathan replied.

The DCI nodded and glanced at Kate. "Good luck," he said, and walked away. DI Mason followed, giving Nathan a disparaging look as he went.

Kate watched them leave and then got a little closer to the body, noticing some strange symbols cut into the bark she didn't recognise. She followed them down to the curious white powder on the ground, which was partially soaking up some of the blood.

"What's that?" She asked, pointing to the white substance on the ground. She wanted to take the conversation away from herself and back to the matter at hand.

"It's salt," said the SOCO woman who was crouched down before the body. She looked up, but only her eyes were visible above the face mask, with her hair under the white coverall's hood.

"Oh, okay," Kate commented.

"Hi, Sheridan," Nathan said. "You SOCO guys have beaten me to the scene again."

"Hey, Nathan. Always. Thought you might be given this one," the SOCO answered him and glanced at Kate.

She took it as an opportunity to introduce herself. "Hi, I'm DC Kate O'Connell."

"Sheridan Lane," the investigator said, with a nod.

"Do we have a cause and time of death?" Nathan asked, ignoring Sheridan's earlier comment.

"We'll know more when we do the full work-up later, but it looks like he's been hung up for a few hours at least, and that he probably died here from that large stab wound on his chest," the Sheridan answered him.

"What happened to his foot?" Kate asked, pointing to the body's left foot which was extended out. It was bloody and possibly chewed.

Sergeant Dyson spoke up. "The dog that found him did that. Chewed on the poor bugger's toes, as if this wasn't bad enough. So, what do you think?" the sergeant asked Nathan. "Looks occult, right?"

Nathan shrugged and began walking around the tree, getting closer to the corpse for a better look. "Maybe, but let's not jump to any conclusions."

Kate followed, peering at the man and the wounds that covered his skin. She noticed Nathan approaching a pile of clothes nearby that had been marked by the investigators. Atop them, beside a dead mobile phone, a wallet lay open, revealing a driver's license. Kate leaned in closer for a better look.

"Jordon Donaldson," she read aloud and peered at the photo. Looking back at the body, she nodded. "So, we know who he is, then."

"Looks that way," Sergeant Dyson replied.

"We'll see if we can get any primary identifiers to match up, but this seems fairly conclusive. I'll check with the SIO. Do we know who Jordan is?" Nathan asked as he pulled out his phone and took a photo of the driver's license.

"Local estate agent, based in Guildford," Dyson said.

"Was someone upset at their valuation?" Kate commented.

"Who knows, that's for you guys to find out. I doubt you'll be short of suspects, though."

"Do we have a home address?" Kate asked.

"Yeah," Sergeant Dyson answered her. "We've requested a Family Support Officer be sent around to the house."

"That'll be our next stop," Nathan said. He was stood up now and looking over the body.

It was always sad to see a life wasted this way, Kate thought. She'd sworn a long time ago to both herself and the memory of her aunt, that she'd try to stop the monsters who committed these kinds of acts from getting away with it.

Jordan looked like he had suffered terribly in his last moments, and Kate could only imagine the fear and the pain he'd been through before release had finally come.

"I'll look forward to your report, Sheridan," Nathan said.

"You'll have it as soon as possible," she answered, before looking over at Kate and nodding. "Nice to meet you."

"And you," Kate answered as she turned to walk with Nathan and the sergeant.

"I'll need a preliminary report on Jordan's body as soon as possible," Nathan said to him, "and try to get into that phone beside the wallet. Let's see what messages he's been sending recently.

"Don't worry, we know what we're doing. So, what do you think?" Sergeant Dyson asked, his tone a little too eager for Kate's liking.

"About what?" Nathan asked.

"The victim, the murder."

"I think someone killed him," Nathan answered.

"I agree, I think he's dead," Kate joined in with a smile.

"Yeah, alright smart arse's, but this is you, Nathan. Dean assigned this one to you for a reason, right?"

"Well, I would guess it's because I'm a detective on the Murder Team?"

"Don't be a nob, we know you well enough by now. Who do you think did it? Satanists?" Dyson seemed to be getting entirely too much joy out of these comments for Kate's liking.

Nathan sighed heavily as they walked along the path, back towards the car park, but didn't reply.

"Really?" Kate said incredulously, stepping in. She almost surprised herself in her early defence of Nathan.

"Leave it, Kate. Thanks for your help, Sergeant, but we really can't discuss any working theories this early in the investigation," Nathan said.

"Alright, have it your way. The dog walker is over there if you want to ask her anything."

"Thanks," Nathan said, and walked over to her, introducing himself and Kate.

"So, we understand you found the body. Can you go through the events of this morning for me?"

CHAPTER 5

"I don't think she had anything to do with this," Nathan said as they drove away from the crime scene, heading towards the outskirts of Guildford.

"Me neither," Kate agreed. "It might be a long time before she goes walking alone in those woods again though."

Nathan nodded. "I'm sorry that this is your first case."

"Why? I'm not," Kate answered him.

"For your first case, this looks like it might be a strange one."

"I don't mind. I mean, I admit, I didn't think people like this killer lived in leafy Surrey, but we have a job to do, no matter what the killer believes."

Nathan nodded. "Oh, they do, people like that are everywhere."

"So I can see. Do you get assigned many of these strange cases?" Kate asked.

"A few," Nathan answered her, sounding cagy.

Kate was beginning to get the feeling that whether warranted or not, Nathan was seen by some of the other officers as something of a conspiracy theorist. She wondered what he'd done to give them that impression.

"So, tell me your initial thoughts on what we've seen so far?" Nathan asked her.

"Alright," she said, and thought about her answer for a moment before replying. "So, I don't think we can say much about the victim yet, other than him being a local businessman, so I guess we'll see how that pans out, but the killing itself is clearly ritualised. Sacrificial, perhaps? There are clear occult influences there, so we're looking for someone with interest in the occult or related fields."

Nathan nodded in agreement. "Good. We'll know a little more when the forensics report and the autopsy come in," he said as they turned into a quiet, picturesque estate that was very much in line with Surrey's affluent middle class and spotted the Police car parked a little way up the road.

"Here we are," Nathan said as he pulled in, and climbed out.

Kate exited the car and followed Nathan onto the driveway of Jordan Donaldson's house. It was a reasonably modern, detached property set back from the road. They had a garden out front and a single car on the driveway, but nothing looked out of place or wrong to Kate's eyes.

Nathan led the way up to the front door and pressed the doorbell. Moments later, it was opened by a uniformed officer as Kate pulled out her warrant card and showed it to her. Nathan did likewise. They were let inside without issue and shown into the front room where two women sat on opposite sofas.

"Detective," Nathan said as a woman in a suit stood and crossed the room to them.

"Nathan," she said in greeting. "Looks like I'm on your team." She nodded to Kate, offering her hand. "DC Faith Evanson, Family Support Officer."

"DC Kate O'Connell," Kate replied, shaking the woman's hand.

"Nice to meet you. Let me introduce you. Joanna?" the detective said to the puffy-eyed woman sat nearby. She'd clearly been crying, and even now her eyes were glassy and wet. She held a tissue, clutching it in both hands. She seemed small and vulnerable sat alone on the sofa as she looked up, clearly still in something of a daze.

"Joanna, these are Detectives Halliwell and O'Connell, they're here to talk to you about Jordan."

Joanna nodded and looked away with a sniff. Her mind was clearly elsewhere, which was quite understandable given the circumstances.

"We'd like to ask you some questions regarding your husband, if that's okay Mrs Donaldson?" Nathan asked.

"Yes, of course. Whatever I can do to help," she said, her eyes darting about as she spoke, as if they were unable to settle on anything.

"Firstly, we'd like to offer our condolences," Kate cut in. "We're sorry for your loss, and we'll do everything we can to bring this case to a close."

Joanna nodded to her with a brief, strained smile. "Thank you."

Kate glanced at Nathan, who nodded to her approvingly, before focusing back on Joanna. "Mrs Donaldson, I have a photo of a driver's license here that was found at the scene. With your permission, I'd like to show it to you so you can confirm that it belongs to your husband, okay?"

Joanna nodded, and Nathan showed her the screen on his phone. Joanna's eyes swam with tears as she gazed at the image, before nodding and looking away to wipe her eyes. "That's him," she said with a sniff.

"Thank you, Mrs Donaldson. Can you tell me a little about your relationship with your husband? Was everything okay?"

Joanna sniffed. "Oh, yes. We were fine. We were looking forward to... to..." She sniffed and took a moment to calm herself. "I'm pregnant," she said finally, her voice cracking. "We were looking forward to having our first. We were happy."

"Oh my gosh, I'm so sorry," Kate replied, a lump forming her her throat at the situation that this poor woman now found herself in. "We don't want to upset you..."

"It's okay," Joanna replied, clearly trying to push these thoughts away and remain composed before herself and Nathan. "Please, continue."

"Are you sure?" Kate asked.

Joanna nodded, wiping her eyes and taking another deep breath.

"You've been together a while?" Kate asked.

Joanna smiled. "We were high school sweethearts. We've been together for years. We'd always planned to have a family, and with Jordan's business going well, we thought now would be a good time..." Joanna's voice cracked with emotion as she let her sentence trail off.

"Of course. Thank you, you're doing well," Kate said with a reassuring smile. Joanna attempted to return it, but it came across as forced, and merely a pleasentry.

After giving Joanna a moment to gather herself Nathan asked, "The pregnancy was a joint decision?" Kate thought it was a rather blunt question, but she could see the value of it.

"Yes, of course. We were thrilled about it." Joanna said, bristling at the implication.

"That's okay, Mrs Donaldson," Kate interjected. "I know these are difficult questions, but we need to get a full picture of everything to do with your husband, including your relationship with him and any recent events that might have an impact on this case."

"I understand," Joanna squeaked.

"Okay, good," Kate replied. "Perhaps you could tell us a little about last night? Where was your husband?"

"He was working late, at the office in town. I went to bed early and when I woke up, he still wasn't home."

"He was at the office?" Kate asked.

"At his business. He runs an estate agency in Guildford. It's doing very well."

"And was he working alone last night?" Nathan asked.

"I... I don't know," she answered, her voice cracking slightly.

"Did he say he was working with anyone?"

"No. He didn't mention anyone."

"Alright," Nathan said. "So what happened this morning?"

"I tried calling his mobile, but there was no answer. I tried the office as well, but no one there has seen him, but apparently his car's still there."

Kate glanced at Nathan, who returned her look, both of them aware of what this might mean.

"There are people there now?" Nathan asked.

"Oh yes, Kay always gets in early."

"Okay. Thank you very much, Mrs Donaldson, we'll be in touch shortly," Nathan said, standing up and pulling his phone out again. He tapped the screen and made for the front door with the phone to his ear.

Kate smiled at Joanna. "Thank you for your help, we'll find whoever did this," she said, and followed Nathan out of the house, catching up to him on the driveway as he spoke on his phone.

"...yes, Donaldson's Estate Agents in Guildford, get a team there now, we need to cordon it off and get the people in there out before they contaminate it any further. No, don't call ahead. I don't want them knowing we're coming, just in case. Yes, we're heading there now."

CHAPTER 6

"Good job in there, Kate," Nathan said, looking over at her as if seeing her in a new light. Kate smiled to herself, getting the feeling that he was warming to her a little bit.

"Thanks. So, what did you think of her?" Kate asked as Nathan sped through the back streets, the lights on the unmarked car flashing.

"Joanna?" Nathan asked. "She seemed upset, but I'd expect nothing less. I don't think there was anything suspicious about what she said."

"I don't know. I'm not so sure."

"Oh? Why?"

"I don't know. I just got a feeling that she was holding something back."

"Like what?"

Kate shrugged. "I'm not sure. Maybe I'm wrong, but it was just a feeling I got when we were talking to her."

"You think this was lying, then?"

"Lying, or just leaving something out maybe. Not telling us everything."

"Well, I'm sure we'll be talking to her again," Nathan said as he made his way through traffic, into the centre of town. It was mid-morning, and while the rush hour was long gone, it was still busy as they moved deeper into the city.

Guildford had several roads running through its main shopping district, some of which were pedestrianised, but Donaldson's Estate Agents was just off one of the streets that cars were allowed to drive along, making their approach a little easier.

They listened as dispatch directed the other cars to the office over the radio, and arrived just as the first marked car pulled up outside.

"You take the lead on this, let's see how you do," Nathan said as they jumped out of the car and made their way up to the office, greeting the uniformed officers as they went.

"I want minimal presence inside the office," Nathan said to the sergeant leading the uniformed team. "This is a possible active crime scene with forensic evidence that we need to preserve. Myself, DC O'Connell, and you two come in, but stay behind us," he said, picking out two of the officers that were approaching the office. Everyone else out here began cordoning off the area and setting up to process the occupants.

Reaching the door, Nathan held it open and let her in first. She pulled her warrant card as she stepped inside to find nine people stood or sat at desks.

"Can I have your attention, please," Kate said, projecting her voice through the property to the back of the room while holding up her identification. "I'm Detective O'Connell with the Surrey Police. I need you all to stop whatever you're doing, pick up only whatever you brought into the office with you today, and make your way to the front. Thank you."

They began to move, standing up from their seats, looking somewhat nervous. A larger woman with dark hair, wearing a dark business skirt and white shirt took a couple of steps forward.

"What's this all about?" the woman asked, her tone tense and professional.

"All you need to know right now is that this is an active crime scene and we need you to leave the building. So, if you wouldn't mind, please, just come forward, and follow the instructions given to you."

"A crime scene?" the woman asked.

Kate nodded and watched the woman's body language shift from confrontational, to something a little less self-assured as she moved back to her desk to grab her things.

Everyone complied and moved towards the front of the office where the uniformed officers began to guide them outside. The woman she'd just spoken to walked over after picking up her handbag and coat.

"Jordan's not here yet, does he know about this?" the woman asked.

"I'm sorry, may I have your name, please?" Kate asked quietly, guiding her to one side of the door to talk to her privately.

"Kay. Kay Seward. Senior Sales Consultant."

"Thank you, Kay, I'm Kate. So, you're in charge here?"

"When Jordan isn't around," she replied. "What's wrong, what's happened to him?"

"Well, you're going to find out anyway, so…" Kate shrugged. "Jordan Donaldson was found dead this morning under suspicious circumstances."

"You mean, he was murdered?" one of the passing employees asked.

"Oh my god," Kay replied, putting her hand to her mouth in shock.

Kate rolled her eyes at having been overheard, and addressed the remaining people in the office. "Please, everyone, make your way outside. The officers outside will need to speak to you and take your details before we can let you leave. We'll be wanting to talk to all of you again very soon."

Kate watched them file out through the front door where the waiting officers began to ask a few questions while taking fingerprints and DNA swabs. She had a good look at each of them as they walked out and noticed one of the girls wearing black with a pentagram on a chain around her neck. The young woman wore dark eye makeup, with black hair that framed her alabaster skin, giving her a slightly gaunt appearance. Kate had seen something like that before and felt sure it was some kind of occult symbol.

Pondering what she'd just seen, Kate watched her walk out and stand with the others who were waiting to speak to the officers.

"So, I heard that right, did I? Jordan's dead? Are you sure you sure that's who it is?" said a voice from in front of her. She turned to see a man who was a good couple of inches shorter than her, but stocky and lean. He clearly worked out. He had a shaved head and wore a jacket and jeans.

"Yeah, we are. I'm sorry," Kate said with a nod.

"That's okay. Well, I mean, it's not. It sucks, but..." The man paused, took an emotion-filled breath, and started again. "I'm Wilson, Wilson Hollins. I own the property. I'm happy to help in any way I can."

"You own it?"

"Jordan leases it from me. I own a few of the units up the high street. We had a meeting scheduled here today. I thought he'd just popped out."

"How come?"

"His car's around the back."

"Oh, I see," she said, glancing over at Nathan who looked back with slightly raised eyebrows. "Well, he won't be attending your meeting, I'm afraid."

"Heh, yeah, I guess not. Shame, nice man. Anyway, thanks Kate. I'll go speak to one of your colleagues."

Kate nodded to him and returned to looking at the girl in black with a frown.

"See something?" Nathan asked, having clearly noticed her expression.

"I'm not sure. Maybe. That girl, she was wearing an occult-looking necklace."

"Occult-looking?"

"A five-pointed star, upside down, inside a circle," Kate explained.

"An inverted pentagram," Nathan commented. "Alright. Make a note of it."

Kate nodded and pulled out her notepad that already had several of her observations about the case scribbled inside. "So, you know a little about the occult then?"

"It's a hobby," he said.

"So, what's it mean?" Kate asked.

Nathan looked at her sideways. "Alright, sure. It used to be used by the Christian faith to represent the five wounds of Christ, but these days it's more commonly associated with Wicca, and Satanism when inverted."

"You mean upside down, like how that girl was wearing it?"

Nathan nodded.

"Okay," Kate answered, noting down a few bullet points in her notepad. She turned to look over the office, which now stood empty apart from herself and Nathan. "Do you think this is where it happened?"

"Maybe. If that really is his car out back, that would add weight to the theory that he'd been attacked here, or taken from the premises somehow."

"Hmm," Kate answered as she looked over the office. Four desks, two on either side of the room stood directly in front of her, with another pair at the back. A door stood open at the back of the room, leading to a hallway and what she guessed were other rooms and offices, but they'd need to get some crime scene suits on to go looking.

"CSI's here," Nathan announced from beside her. She looked out front again to see a SOCO van pull up onto the kerb at the end of the short pedestrianized street. "Let's get suited up and have a look around."

A few minutes later, Kate wore a white crime scene suit with covers for her shoes and blue latex gloves as she stepped back into the office with Nathan, who was similarly dressed.

The SOCO officers had already begun to move through the premises, and there were several of them in the front of the office, picking over the desks and workstations, taking photos and video.

Nothing stood out as being out of place on the main office floor, and Kate was keen to get a look out back. She walked through with Nathan into the rear corridor that had a small kitchenette immediately on their right. The kettle was still hot and steaming with empty mugs sat on the counter, but again, nothing seemed out of place. Further back they found a toilet, a storage room filled mainly with boxes of files, a meeting room, and an office with the name Jordan Donaldson stencilled onto the glass set into the door.

Inside, a Scene Of Crime Officer stood over the desk, carefully picking up a small square of black card by the edges and turning it over. The man recoiled from the item in his hand and looked up upon hearing Nathan and Kate walk inside.

"You'd better take a look at this," the SOCO said.

Kate followed Nathan over to the desk, and moved around the opposite side, flanking the investigator.

"So, I found this face down on here, like this," the man explained, showing them the back of the square card. It was glossy black, with grey sections at the top and bottom. The brand of a photographic company emblazoned across it.

"So, I turned it over, after I photographed the desk," the investigator continued, flipping the item over to reveal it was a Polaroid, complete with the white border around the image.

An emaciated, bloodied, and bruised face stared out at them from the image, and below it, written in black marker were the words, '*4 days*'.

"Who is that?" Kate asked, noting there were some blood splatters on the image-side of the photo.

"I don't know," Nathan said.

Kate peered a little closer at the photo. "It looks like he's alive. See, he's looking at the camera. I don't know. There's something familiar about this man," Kate wondered out loud.

"Familiar? Have you seen him before?"

"I'm not sure. Maybe, yeah. I feel like I should know who he is. This has to have been left by the killer, right?"

"That would be my assumption, but we'll need to eliminate the office workers first. We'll have to search their properties. Alright, well, our first priority is finding out this man's identity," Nathan said and used his phone to snap a quick photo of the Polaroid.

"We'll run tests on the blood, see if we get a match," the investigator said, slipping the photo into an evidence bag.

"Good. Send us the report as soon as you have something."

Kate stood up straight and looked around the room. "Four days. That's not very clear, is it? I mean, four days from when? Yesterday? Today?"

"We should assume yesterday, making it a shorter timeframe."

Kate could see his logic. "Good thinking, Batman," she commented as she scanned over the office once more. "Do you think the room looks like it's been cleaned up."

"I guess," Nathan replied. "But was it cleaned by the killer, a cleaner, or one of the employees who didn't realise they were tampering with a crime scene?"

"I'll let forensics figure that one out," Kate commented.

Nathan nodded to her. "Very wise, Padawan."

"Pada-what?" Kate asked.

"Hmm? Oh, Padawan. It's a Star Wars thing... You know what, forget it," he replied, shaking his head.

Kate laughed. She was enjoying teasing him.

"Let's check the car out and leave the experts to do their job," Nathan said as he walked out nodding to the SOCO who'd been in the room with them.

Stepping out the back of the office, a single car stood waiting for them with a uniformed officer stood nearby. Kate moved around the car and peered into the windows without touching them, but again, there was nothing obviously suspect that she could make out through the tinted side windows on Jordan's BMW.

"Nothing much to see out here," Kate said.

"No," Nathan agreed, as he pulled his phone out of his pocket to check a message.

Kate looked around while Nathan read the message on his phone. They were stood in a wide, but not very deep, area that ran along behind the row of shops and was clearly used for loading and as a parking area for workers. One unit further up, was a cut-through back to the road that looked like it was the main access point to this back-lot area.

"Anything relevant?" Kate asked, noticing that Nathan had finished reading the message.

"The preliminary report on the body is in, and it looks like we have Jordan's phone records as well. They're back at the station."

"Alright, shall we head back?"

Nathan nodded. "I'll call ahead, let the DCI know about the photo. That should get us some more resources."

CHAPTER 7

Kate walked back into the Murder Team's office, crossed to her desk, and put her things down while Nathan removed his jacket. Kate was shrugging out of her own coat when a woman in plainclothes strode over.

"Sir? We've just had word from the Pathologyst that Jordan's dental records match up with the body. The SIO's confirmed he's satisfied that we've identified the body."

Nathan looked up and smiled. "Thanks, Debby," he answered her. "Kate, this is Debby Constable, she's one of our desk clerks."

"Hi, Debby," Kate said with a smile. "Nice name."

"Hey. Yeah, I'm the one constable that isn't," she answered. Kate laughed as Debby retreated back to her desk.

"Alright, let's have a look at what we've got, shall we?" Nathan said. Kate pulled up her chair and sat down beside Nathan as he logged into his computer and navigated to the preliminary report on the body of Jordan Donaldson. The statement was brief and outlined the main visible wounds on his body. Right now, it looked like Jordan was killed by a deep stab wound to the chest that hit his heart, but there were lots of other cuts all over his body that had contributed to a large amount of blood loss. The report also noted bruising around his neck, and what looked like a single puncture mark on his right shoulder.

"What do you make of that?" Nathan asked, clearly curious as to her thoughts.

Kate sat back and brought her hand up to her chin in thought. "Well, a puncture wound suggests that he might have been injected with something, and the bruising on the neck suggests strangulation. But it looks like Jordan was killed by the stab wound. So, I'd guess that he was subdued by someone getting him in an armlock around his neck, before injecting him with some kind of anaesthetic while he was out cold."

Nathan nodded. "That's basically what I was thinking. Also, given that he was apparently at his work last night, I think he might have been attacked in the office."

Kate agreed. "Jordan's car still being there, and the photo on his desk only adds weight to that idea, as well. So, they got in somehow," Kate continued, "subdued him, injected him, and then moved him to the woods where they killed him. But not before leaving us that cryptic note."

"That feels right to me," Nathan said. "I'll put in a request for any CCTV in the road out front of the office. Maybe we'll get lucky."

"Were there any security cameras in the office itself?" Kate asked.

"I don't know. I didn't see any, but maybe the forensics team will find something."

"We can only hope," Kate replied as Nathan then navigated to another folder on the system, listed as Jordan's Mobile Records, and opened it up.

Inside was a list of phone calls made from the device, as well as message threads, including the most recent ones between him and his wife, and someone called Naomi. A quick read through the last couple of messages made it clear that Naomi was a work colleague at the office, and in the last message to her, they discussed working late together on the night of Jordan's murder.

"Well, that confirms he was working late, but it looks like he wasn't alone."

"Was Naomi one of the people at the office today, do we know?" Kate asked.

"Good question. I'll chase her up and see if we can get her brought in," Nathan said as Kate spotted DCI Dean walking over to them. "Sir," she said in greeting as he approached.

"So, give me a brief rundown of what's happened," he said, sitting on the edge of a desk across the way.

"So, we have the body of Jordan Donaldson found in the woods between Shere and Horsley early this morning. We believe he was tortured and murdered at the scene, but we think he was kidnapped from his office in Guildford. We spoke to Jordan's wife, Joanna Donaldson who informed us that Jordan had worked late last night and had not returned home. The office is currently being looked at by SOCO's, but we found a Polaroid there that had been left on Jordan's desk."

"Polaroid?" the DCI asked. "What decade is this again?"

"You can get modern Polaroid cameras these days," Kate interjected. "I have one."

"You're not the killer, are you?" the DCI asked, one eyebrow raised.

Kate laughed. "I don't think so."

"Good, then all we need to do is find the one other person in the country who uses Polaroid, and we're done. Case closed."

"I'll bear that in mind, sir," Nathan replied.

"So, what was on this photo?" the DCI continued, suddenly serious again.

Nathan pulled out his phone and showed the photo he'd taken of it, to the DCI. "Here, take a look."

"Four days? Four days until what? Is this a threat against this man's life?"

"I assume so," Nathan replied.

"Do we know who he is?" he asked, pointing to the image.

"No. But there was blood on the photo, so maybe that will shed some light on it."

"Then, you have your deadline. We need to find the murderer before he kills again," DCI Dean said.

"We're on it," Nathan replied.

"I know you are. Any resources you need, just ask. Alright?"

"Yes, sir," Nathan replied.

"Okay, carry on, keep me updated," he said and left them to their work.

"Alright, while we wait for some results, we might as well start getting onto the paperwork and writing up our initial reports."

Kate nodded and wheeled her seat back to her desk where she logged into her computer and set work, starting with changing her password to something she'd remember.

Paperwork was a necessary evil, and the part of the job Kate did not enjoy. It was also absolutely vital as a case progressed, became more complex, and eventually made it to court. It was not worth putting in all that effort to apprehend a criminal only to have them get off on a technicality later because she'd omitted something key from her reports.

The next couple of hours moved slowly and were only interrupted by her lunch and Nathan informing her that Naomi had indeed been at the office this morning and was coming in to be interviewed.

"So, what do you think the relationship is between these two?" Kate asked.

"I take it you think Jordan and Naomi were more than work colleagues, then?" Nathan said.

"I think Jordan was squeezing a few extra benefits out of his working life, sure," Kate replied. "Maybe things weren't quite as rosy at home as Joanna was making out."

"Do you think that's what you were picking up on when you said you thought something was off with his wife?"

"My instinct is taking me that way. Maybe Jordan wasn't as keen on the pregnancy as Joanna was, and went looking for something a little more fun elsewhere."

"Well, there's nothing incriminating so far, just circumstantial evidence, and all the messages on the phone looked purely professional. Friendly, but professional."

"I guess we'll find out when Naomi comes in," Kate mused.

Nathan smiled. "I guess so."

Kate went back to her work, writing up her notes and findings and what they had worked on so far today. It was mind-numbing work, and she'd been sipping on a coffee that Nathan had brought to her a little while ago.

Kate took another sip, but it was cold and the taste of it made her shiver. She'd spotted where the break room was a little earlier and decided it was time to go investigate it for herself. Besides, it was getting late in the afternoon, and she needed the caffeine.

She offered to get another drink for Nathan, but he declined the offer, continuing with his own small mountain of paperwork, while Kate navigated around the desks.

Located off to one side, the break room had a work surface with a kettle, microwave, and a fridge at one end, and a sink and draining board up the other. Three small circular tables stood lined up along the middle of the room, surrounded by chairs.

As she approached, she heard two people talking inside, and slowed to listen in before they spotted her.

"I'm going to recommend he takes them off the case," the male voice said. "It's too big for the weirdo and his rookie now that it looks like we have a serial killer on the loose."

"A-hem," a female voice replied as Kate stepped into the room.

Two detectives sat at a nearby table—DI Mason, who she'd seen following the DCI around, and a woman.

Kate smiled at them as she walked in. "Hey," she said.

The woman—a tall, stocky lady who Kate guessed to be in her forties—got up and approached her.

"Hi. I'm Claire, nice to meet you," she said, offering her hand to Kate.

Kate took it and shook it firmly. "Kate. Kate O'Connell," she answered and pointed to the coffee jar. "Can I make you something?"

"No, thanks, I've just had one. But let me offer you one of these," she said and pulled open a Tupperware box on the side to reveal several cupcakes covered in white icing. There were only a few left and plenty of crumbs covering the base of the box.

"Oooh, lovely" Kate said with a smile as she plucked one from inside. "Thanks."

"No problem. I love baking, I'll have something else tomorrow."

"She's our resident dealer in sugary treats," Mason said from behind Claire. "She's got us all hooked. Don't know what we'd do if she ever got transferred."

"That's Sam," Claire said, glancing back at him.

"Yeah, we've met." Sam got up and walked over, also offering his hand. "Sam Mason. Nice to meet you."

"Kate," she replied and shook his hand, making sure to get a good grip.

"How's your first day going?" Sam asked with a curious smile.

"Eventful," Kate answered truthfully. "I did not expect this on day one."

"I bet Nathan's loving it, isn't he? Finally, something juicy to sink his teeth into. So, what's the theory this time? Aliens? The Loch Ness Monster on holiday down south?"

"Don't be horrible," Claire cut in.

"What? We all know what he's like with his conspiracy theories. It's only right that Kate should know about him."

Claire smiled, but it was a fake one. "He's harmless, and a good detective, Sam."

"If you say so."

"Sounds like he's got something of a reputation," Kate commented.

"Nathan has been with the force for a long time," Claire said, "and he does have certain theories about what is really going on, you know, in the halls of power, I guess."

"Just say it as it is. He's a conspiracy theorist," Sam added.

"So that's why we got this case, then?" Kate said.

"Strange one, is it?" Claire asked.

"Some occult influences in the killing," Kate explained.

"You just hope he doesn't screw this one up. You don't want him ruining your career before it's even started. Look, I gotta get on. I'll see you later, Claire. Take care of yourself, Kate, and watch him. Don't let this rookie posting mess things up for you."

Kate nodded and watched Sam walk off before turning back to Claire. "What was all that about?"

Claire offered her a conciliatory smile. "Nathan used to run a Murder Squad. He was a DCI, you know. He's a talented detective with a flair for solving cases, but because of his belief in certain conspiracies, he ended up screwing up a major investigation. The main suspect walked free, and no one was convicted for the murder. Nathan got demoted for his actions on that case, but they kept him around as a DS…"

"Because he was otherwise good at his job?"

Claire nodded. "He was on desk duty for a while, before be began helping on various cases with the team. He's been working alone on some random crap for a while too, but this is the first time he's led an investigation in years. I suppose he's earned it, but he's got a certain reputation for his beliefs, and the rookies usually get partnered with him when they first join the team as a test."

"Like me," Kate answered.

"Like you," Claire answered, inclining her head. "Rachel over there was his partner before you."

Kate looked into the room to see the dark-haired woman Claire was pointing out to her. She was a little older than Kate, maybe, but not by much.

"He's not mentioned any conspiracy stuff to me yet."

Claire smiled. "Give it time, it'll rear its head at some point."

"Okay, well, thanks for the heads-up," Kate said.

"Look, Sam has a pretty harsh view of Nathan. He's more of a 'by the book' type and doesn't like Nathan's more unorthodox approach. The conspiracy thing is just the icing on the cake really, so don't let Sam get to you. Nathan really is good at his job."

"He seems to be."

Claire nodded. "You're enjoying working with him, then?"

Kate looked across the office at Nathan where he sat, hunched over his computer, engrossed in his work. "Yeah, I guess so. I mean, it's early days, and I've only been with him today, but he knows his stuff."

Claire smiled. "Alright then, I guess I'll let you get on with it. Enjoy the cake," she said and left the break room.

Kate watched her go and looked over the office and the dynamic that was clearly at work here.

She was the newbie on the team, and it looked like they were always posted with Nathan, probably as a hazing ritual of some kind to see how they got on. But honestly, Kate didn't have anything against Nathan. As far as she could see, he was a diligent and keen-minded detective who knew what it took to get the job done.

It sounded like he had a few skeletons in his closet, but then, he wasn't the only one with a past that he wanted to forget.

With a shrug, she walked back to her desk and sat back down at her computer, sipping her new, hot mug of coffee.

She was halfway through her next drink when she heard Nathan pick up the phone behind her.

"Yes? Okay, thanks," he said down the line. Kate turned to him.

"What's up?"

"Naomi's here, she's in interview room three," he replied, standing up. "Let's go see what she's got to say for herself.

Kate followed Nathan downstairs to the interview rooms where an officer showed them to the one with Naomi in it.

She sat behind a table in the room and looked up as they walked in.

"I came as quick as I could. If there's anything I can do to help..." she said.

"Hopefully there is," Kate said. "This is an interview which will be conducted under caution plus three. You are under caution, which I will recite to you. During this interview, you do not have to say anything. But it may harm your defence if you do not mention when questioned, something which you later rely on in court. Anything you do say may be given in evidence. Do you understand?"

"I think so, yes," Naomi replied.

"In addition, you have the right to free legal advice, should you decide you want it, you're not under arrest or anything, and you can leave at any time." Kate finished. "Now that the legal part is out the way, we just have a few questions about last night, if that's okay?"

Naomi nodded. "Do I need a lawyer or anything?"

"You shouldn't need one, no, but say so if you want to request one, alright?" Naomi was a good looking girl, Kate thought, with her long dark hair and pretty face. She wasn't shy about showing off a little cleavage either.

Had she turned Jordan's eye? Attracted him in and got involved with him? She certainly would attract a few admiring glances walking around dressed like that.

Taking their seats opposite her, Kate looked over at Nathan, who nodded for her to continue as he readied his notepad.

"It's Naomi Sawyer, right?" Kate asked.

"That's right."

"So, how would you describe your relationship with Mr Donaldson?"

"Um, well I guess it's employer and employee. I work for him," Naomi answered.

"At the Estate Agency?"

Naomi nodded.

"So, it's purely professional then?"

"Well, I guess we're friends too, but that's all. We went to school together years ago, but I'd not seen him in years until I went to apply for this job. It was good to see him again after so long."

"So you're friends?"

"I guess. I mean. We were. We only really see each other at work now... I mean, we did..." she answered, her calm demeanour showing the first signs of cracking as she fought her emotions.

"Did you sometimes work late with Mr Donaldson?"

"Sometimes. A few of us did. It depended on who was available."

"And you were available last night?"

Naomi nodded, as tears budded in the corners of her eyes.

"It's okay, we can take a break at any time you want," Kate offered.

"No, no, it's fine. I'm fine," she answered with a sniff.

"Okay. So, you worked with Jordan last night?"

"No. I mean, I tried. I went to the office to meet him. I hadn't worked there during the day yesterday. It was my day off. But he asked if I was free to help him, so I went over. No one was in though. The place was locked up, and no one answered."

"You didn't see any movement or any lights on inside?"

"No, nothing. I knocked and rang the doorbell for a while."

"Can you confirm the time you went there?"

"Yeah, it was about seven forty-five, eight o'clock. Around there, I think."

"Can anyone corroborate this for you?"

Naomi shrugged. "I live alone and didn't tell anyone what I was doing. There's a camera on the street though, I think. Can you check them?"

"We're in the process of obtaining CCTV from the area," Nathan cut in.

Naomi nodded. "You know, it was strange because his car was there like it usually is, but he wasn't in the office. So, I guess someone... You know..." she said, stumbling over her words as a lump formed in her throat.

Kate nodded. "Okay, so you're sure you didn't see him yesterday, at all?"

Naomi shook her head. "Sorry, no."

"Do you know his wife, Joanna at all?" Nathan asked.

"She's been to the office a few times. We've swapped a few pleasantries. That's all, really. I don't really know her that well. Kay knows her better."

"We'll be speaking with Kay soon. What about any of your other colleagues, have you noticed any of them acting strangely? Have any of them fallen out with Mr Donaldson recently?"

Naomi thought for a moment, creasing her brow, before shaking her head. "Sorry, no. Everyone was getting on with Jordan just fine, as far as I know anyway."

Kate sat forward again, putting her arms on the table. "Who has access to the property? Who has a key?"

"Um, well Jordan, obviously. Kay has a key, and I think Hunter does as well."

"That's Hunter West, correct?" Kate asked, checking her notes.

"That's right. He's close with Jordan. They're mates and go drinking together sometimes."

Kate nodded and made a note of Naomi's opinion. "What about um, Robyn Boyce is it? The girl in Black. How well do you know her?"

"Robyn? She's nice, I guess," she answered, shrugging. "She's quiet, keeps to herself. You know the type."

"Sure," Kate answered, thinking to herself that it was always the quiet ones you had to watch.

Nathan spoke up with a new line of questioning. "I have some notes here that say you reported your former husband, Steve

Brewster for harassment three times following your separation, and once again after your divorce. The last time was a little under a year ago."

Naomi nodded. Kate noticed her body language changing again as if shutters had suddenly descended.

"Has there been any further harassment since?"

"No," Naomi answered her, her voice clipped. This was a subject that she didn't like to talk about. At the very least, it sounded like there were bad memories there.

"Are you sure?"

"I'm sure," Naomi answered him.

"Does he know about your new job?" Kate asked, seeing where Nathan was going with this.

Naomi shook her head. "I... don't think so. I've not told him. I don't even know where he lives anymore. He could be in Scotland, for all I know."

"You're certain about that?"

Naomi nodded.

"What about photography. Are you into photography? Taking Polaroids maybe?"

Naomi shook her head in confusion.

"What about Steve?"

"No," Naomi replied, the very idea of that clearly sounding ridiculous to her.

"Is there anything else you wish to tell us?" Nathan asked.

"I don't think so," Naomi answered him. "But if you have any more questions, I'm happy to answer them."

Kate caught Nathan's glance, silently asking her if she had any other questions. Kate gave a slight shake of her head and a shrug of her shoulders, indicating that she didn't.

"Alright, then. Thank you, Miss Sawyer, for coming in today, you've been very helpful," Nathan finished.

Leaving the interview room behind, another officer led Naomi Sawyer out while Kate and Nathan made their way back upstairs.

"So, you did some digging on her, did you?" Kate asked.

"Sorry, I just found that out before I got the phone call that she was here. I didn't have time to share it with you before going in."

Kate nodded. "Understood. But can we keep each other in the loop from now on?"

"Of course. Sorry. I'm used to working alone most of the time."

Kate nodded. "That's okay, I understand."

"Let's finish up, it's way past the end of your shift anyway. I'm getting a series of interviews lined up for tomorrow with everyone who was in the office. We need to know a little more about these people."

"We're not working into the small hours on this?" she asked.

Nathan smiled. "It's your first day, you've already put in some overtime, but I need you fresh for tomorrow. Besides, the night shift can continue some of the work we've been doing."

"Are you leaving too?" she asked, getting the feeling that she knew what the answer would be.

"No, I'll stay on a little longer, and I'll see you tomorrow, alright?" Kate's suspicions had been right, he wasn't finishing up just yet.

"Okay, if you're sure," Kate answered, as she noticed DCI Dean walking over to her with DI Mason in tow. "Sir?" she said in greeting.

"O'Connell. Nathan. Is it going well?"

"We're making progress, sir," Nathan replied.

"Send today's report over to Mason and I, will you?"

"I'll finish it up and send it over now. I'm sending Kate home, though. Her shift's over.

"Good idea, don't want the rookie getting burnout on the first day," the DCI replied.

"I'm fine, I can manage," Kate replied.

"I know you can. Your record is exemplary, but you've already worked longer than you should today," he explained, checking the time on his watch. "You're more useful to us refreshed and awake though."

"As you wish, sir," Kate replied, feeling a little deflated that she was being sent home, but she understood his reasoning.

"Kate, do you have a moment before you head home?" the DCI asked.

"Of course. I'll see you tomorrow, Nathan," she said with a smile and followed the DCI back to his office, where she had started her first day on the job. She sat opposite him again as he leant forward onto his desk with a friendly expression on his face.

"So, how was your first day?" he asked.

"Very productive, sir. Getting assigned a case like this on my first day was a little daunting, but I think Nathan and I are working well together."

"So, no worries or concerns?"

"Well, the way this case is being run is a little unorthodox sir, but if you're okay with it?"

Malcolm Dean leant forward, putting his arms on the desk. "I understand. Look, Nathan is a skilled detective. He knows what he's doing. He used to have my job, before…"

"I know. Claire told me."

Malcolm nodded. "Good. So this case should play to his strengths. It should also give you a chance to shine, provided Nathan doesn't go off the rails again."

"I'm sure he won't."

"Do your duty, that's all you can do, and tell me if he goes off on some wild tangent. I can protect you if need be, make sure he doesn't take your career down with him."

"I'm certain that won't happen."

DCI Dean smiled. "I'm sure it won't either. I'm being overcautious. So, other than that, is everything okay?"

"Yes, sir, I'm quite happy, not sure DI Mason is though."

"Hmmm. I know about Mason. He's had issues with Nathan for a while, but I know Nathan better than he does. Nathan might have some strange ideas about the world, but he is a skilled detective. He'll do a good job on this, as will you, I'm sure."

Kate smiled. "Thank you for the vote of confidence, sir. I'll do my best."

"Excellent. You can come speak to me at any time. I know Nathan can be difficult sometimes."

Kate smiled. "Seriously, it's fine. He's a pussycat, really."

The DCI raised his eyebrows at her comment. "Is that right?"

"Maybe don't tell him I said so, sir."

"Sure thing. Alright, you're free to go. Get some rest, you've got a long day ahead of you tomorrow."

CHAPTER 8

It was dark outside again, he realised as he woke up, his body stiff and in pain. He'd lost track of the days a long time ago.

At least, it felt like it was a long time ago. Maybe it wasn't. Maybe it was only a few nights. He couldn't be sure. It all blended into one, like some kind of horrific nightmare that there was no waking up from.

He was in constant pain. Everything ached. His wrists and ankles were sore, rubbed red and raw from the unforgiving metal cuffs that held him spread-eagled to the bed. Even if he could lift his head, which he doubted was possible it hurt so much, he didn't want to look down at his body.

He didn't like to think about what that monster had done to him. The thought of the torture alone was enough to reduce him to a quivering wreck or make him vomit up the little food that had been given to him.

He was hungry the whole time, and there was a constant ache in his gut. He couldn't be sure if that was the effect of his hunger or the injuries that his captor had inflicted upon him.

Mark closed his eyes, shutting out the view of the stained ceiling he knew so well, which seemed to taunt his every waking moment.

He remembered the screams and shouts from the other room. When had that been? Recently. He was sure of that.

When he'd first heard the sounds of movement, when his captor had presumably dragged what Mark felt sure was another victim into the building, he'd thought he was being rescued.

He called out in desperate, blind panic. Shouting to get attention, as much as his ruined body would allow.

But it had been no use.

Later came the screams. He'd been woken up by them. They came from another room somewhere nearby after his captor had left the building.

The man's words were slurred, unintelligible, but Mark had called out all the same. He'd tried to get a name, but couldn't be sure if he'd heard correctly.

Jaden? Jordan? Jason? It could have been any of those.

Then his captor had returned and hurt the man before either killing or removing the him from the building. Mark didn't know which, but the screaming had stopped.

And he was alone again.

"Good evening, Mark. How are we today?" came the all too familiar voice of his captor and the sound of his footsteps on the hard floor as he approached.

Mark tensed, knowing what was coming.

"The time draws near, my friend. The time of your great sacrifice and my ascension. Ah, yes. It will be glorious. Truly glorious. But as you know, Mark, all great works require time and dedication. They require much work in order to come to fruition. Failing to prepare means preparing to fail. You've heard that little phrase before, right?"

Mark glanced up at the dark figure that loomed above him.

"A masterpiece requires sacrifice, doesn't it Mark? And that's where you come in."

A shiver ran down Mark's spine at those words, and he knew he looked scared.

Above him, the man lifted the camera to his face and snapped another photo, just as he had done the previous day.

"Don't be afraid, my friend. You're in good hands," the man said, putting the camera down and raising a gleaming blade into view. "So, let's get to work, shall we?"

Mark screamed as the pain redoubled, but no one heard him.

CHAPTER 9

Turning into the village of Horsley, having fought her way through morning traffic, Kate immediately noticed several vans poorly parked along the sides of the roads. There were some in the hotel car park opposite the station, and more down the right turn of the upcoming corner. She spotted the usual logos of local and national news organisations on the sides of the vehicles and rolled her eyes.

The word was out, it seemed.

Pulling into the station's car park, Kate saw the crowd of people outside the building. A third of them held bulky cameras, the others held microphones of one kind or another and were milling about, taking notes, or delivering speeches to a camera.

The reporters eyed Kate's hatchback like a school of hungry piranhas as she passed them, no doubt looking for their next victim to rip to shreds.

She hadn't had much direct experience with the press, having been rank and file for the most part, but she guessed that now she was part of a partnership leading an investigation, it was probably kind of inevitable that she'd run into the press more often.

She hadn't felt nervous coming into work today like she had yesterday, the apprehensiveness of the new posting having long since passed. Seeing these reporters though, brought it crashing back onto her shoulders as she tried to mentally prepare herself for the walk into the building.

A couple of deep breaths later, she climbed out of her vehicle and locked it, turning to face the building, only to find a couple of the reporters already approaching her.

"Miss, are you a detective here?"

"Can we ask you a few questions about the death of Jordan Donaldson?"

Fixing her gaze at a point on the ground a short distance ahead of her, Kate strode towards the building, ignoring their questions.

"What can you tell us about Mr Donaldson's death, Detective?"

"Are the reports of occult influences accurate?"

She pressed on, walking through the small crowd, approaching the doors and the relief of escape from their questions.

"Do you have any suspects?"

"Is this killing linked to the disappearance of Mark Summers?"

This last question caught her a little off guard, and she glanced back at the man who asked it as she pushed open the door to the building. An intense looking man with slicked-back blonde hair fixed her with his steely gaze. He was quite striking in appearance. Kate recognised him from TV and knew his reputation, without having to read the press badge that hung around his neck.

Chester Longstaff. A man who she'd heard a few officers talk about in a range of tones. Some spoke highly of him, but most disliked him intensely. He was, according to many, a weaselly little slimeball who always knew entirely too much and wasn't against any tactic to get the story he wanted.

Chester noticed her look, and she caught the slightest smarmy grin on his face before she was through and free of them.

She made her way up to the Murder Team's incident room, and while she wasn't the first in for their shift, she wasn't the last either.

Nathan, however, had beaten her in and was already at his desk, working on his computer.

"Morning," Kate said as she approached their little corner of the room where she noticed a free-standing whiteboard had been set up with photos and notes about the case stuck to it. "Did you go home last night?"

"Briefly," he replied.

"You've been busy, I see."

"I've not got anything better to do really, so why not? There's always paperwork that needs filling, and investigators that need directing. I've got some uniforms doing some door to door and looking into the Estate Agents, just in case it flags anything up."

"You should have said, I would have been in earlier, and maybe missed the guys outside."

Nathan smiled. "Survived them, did you?"

"Got nipped a couple of times, but I made it through."

"Heh. Well, some of them were here when I arrived, but I imagine it's worse now."

"It's pretty bad, yeah."

"Hmmm, might see if we can take the back way out."

"Good idea. So, how do they know about this?" Kate asked.

"Our media office put out a brief statement yesterday, but it's likely someone probably leaked a few extra details to them."

"Money talks," Kate said with a shrug. She'd yet to be approached by the press asking for information in exchange for money, but she knew it happened. Given the pay that a police officer—even a detective—got, she wasn't surprised that some supplemented that income with pay-outs from the press.

Still, she wondered about the conscience and morals of the officers that did that kind of thing.

"We've had reports of them at Joanna Donaldson's house as well, so we put an officer outside to keep them at bay," Nathan stated.

"Good plan," Kate replied as she settled into her seat. She looked up at the board and the happy smiling photo of Jordan Donaldson they had pulled from somewhere online. It contrasted starkly against the shots of the crime scene next to it and his strung up corpse. Kate sucked in a breath of air-conditioned oxygen, pulled a sticky note from the pad on her desk, and stuck it over the image of Jordan's body.

No need to show it off to the whole office.

"Sleep well?" Nathan asked her as she retook her seat.

"Fine, all things considered," she answered as she noticed DS Claire Watson walking over.

"Good morning. How are you?" Claire asked her.

Kate smiled back, warmly. "Hi. Yeah, good thanks. You?"

"Yeah, great. Just to let you know, there are cakes in the break room. Help yourself."

"Oooh, excellent. Thank you," Kate replied as she noticed Claire glance over at Nathan with a wary expression on her face.

"Nathan," she muttered in greeting.

"DS Watson," Nathan replied with a nod, and little in the way of good humour.

Kate watched the small interaction with interest, remembering her conversation with Claire and Sam in the break room, and got the feeling that Claire didn't usually come over to tell Nathan about what she'd been baking or to offer him any.

Claire smiled back at Kate, her expression immediately warmer and bid her good day as she stepped away. Kate smiled to herself, pleased that she had initiated some kind of contact between Nathan and the rest of the office. She made a mental note to make sure she had one of Claire's cakes, and make sure Claire saw her have it. She wanted to encourage that kind of friendly contact.

Kate logged into her PC and started to review the updates on the case and the actions the HOLMES system was suggesting.

"Going to keep me informed today, are you?" said a male voice from nearby.

Kate turned to see DI Mason stood a short distance from their two desks.

"Of course," Nathan replied to him.

Mason nodded and looked over their desks, and then at the Big Board. "Can't say I approve of this being out in the office."

"Assign us an incident room and we'll move it," Nathan answered.

"Do you think this team is made of money?" Mason replied. "We might be in a shiny new building, but we only have a few rooms available. You know how the budget is."

"Then this area here is our MIR, and we need a crazy wall," Nathan said, nodding to the whiteboard.

"Crazy's right," DI Mason replied, the insinuation clear in his voice as he looked at Nathan.

Kate sighed. "Alright boys, stop waving your cocks about, comparing sizes."

Sam looked over at her, a little shocked by her words.

"We'll keep you informed DI Mason, you have my word," Kate assured him.

Sam Mason's eyes narrowed as he looked at her. "Alright, let's see how this goes. I'm watching you," he finished, looking at Nathan before turning and swanning off back to his desk.

Nathan gave a mocking salute as he walked away and then relaxed into his chair. "Ballsy," he said, and then looked back at her with a wicked grin. "I like it."

"You like balls?" Kate quipped back at him.

Nathan rolled his eyes. "So, I meant to ask," Nathan said, swivelling his chair around to face her, and glancing up at the post-it note on the board. "At the crime scene yesterday, you seemed to come over a little ill, or upset. Are you squeamish at all?"

"No, no. Nothing like that," she replied as she cast about for an answer that didn't involve explaining her past to him. "I... I think it was just some first day nerves, you know? Everything just built up, and a murder on my first day just made me feel a little light-headed, that's all. Nothing to worry about."

"Alright. As long as that's all it is."

"Seriously, I'm fine. Don't worry, it was nothing," she insisted, but looked away, not wanting to meet his gaze at that moment while she hunted for a way to change the subject. "Any news on that photo?"

"Actually, yes, there is. The blood tests threw up a DNA match. Mark Summers," Nathan explained and paused as he let that information sink in.

Kate frowned. "Mark Summers?" she asked, trying to place the name. It felt familiar. And then it clicked. "The man who was kidnapped three weeks ago?"

Nathan smiled. "That's him," he replied and showed her a side-by-side comparison of the Polaroid and a photo of Mark taken in a pub looking happy and relaxed.

"So it is. I knew I'd seen his face before. So, what's happening with his case?"

"The skipper has been in touch with their SIO and has arranged for them to send over what they know. We'll do the same, but they'll stay separate cases for now. We'll probably bring them in on this if we find any concrete links to Mark's whereabouts."

"Do you think Mark and Jordan knew one another?" Kate asked.

"I don't know. I've asked the officers on his case to check, so I guess we'll find out."

"Are we not going to speak with Mark's family at all?"

"We could, but the officers on that case already have a rapport with Mark's family, so I'm leaving that side of things up to them for now."

"Sure, I understand. So, more interviews today, then?"

"That's right. We need to talk to the people at the Estate Agency and see what shakes loose," Nathan answered.

Kate got up and approached the board to look at the photos tacked up of all the people who either worked at the office or had been there yesterday morning. Their names were listed beneath each photo.

Kate's eyes scanned over the images, lingering on Naomi Sawyer, Robyn Boyce, and Kay Seward.

"I'm not sure I believe Naomi about her relationship with Jordan being purely professional," Kate said as she looked at the pretty brunette's photo.

"Me neither. I think something's going on there."

Kate nodded. "Old high school friends meeting up years later when his wife's fallen pregnant? I'd happily bet money on them having an affair. It's too convenient."

"But why lie?" Nathan asked. "If Naomi was shagging him, why wouldn't she tell us? It only incriminates her if she's not being honest."

Kate shrugged. "I'm not sure. I guess we need to keep digging."

"We will. I've got some officers trying to find Steve, Naomi's ex."

"Good call. If Jordan and Naomi were having an affair, do you think Joanna knows about it?"

"I don't know. Probably not," Nathan answered her.

"I'm not so sure. I think she might have known," Kate said.

"Then she lied to us too."

Kate nodded. "So how many people do we have to speak to?"

"Six. Kay, Hunter, Chris, Darcy, Robyn who all work at the office, and the property owner, Wilson. We'll get statements from the two customers who were in there yesterday as well."

"That's a lot to fit in. Can we get some help?"

"Way ahead of you."

***

"Alright, thanks for helping with this," Nathan said to DC Rachel Arthur, who had joined them at their desks.

"No problem. I read up on the case. Makes a change and gets me out of the office," she answered with a smile. "Good to work with you again, too."

"Jealous?" Nathan replied.

Rachel smiled. "Oh, but of course. You know I do nothing but sit over there and pine for you all day long."

"I'd suspected as much. DI Burnham not doing it for you?"

Rachel raised an eyebrow as she continued to smile. "Now that would be telling, wouldn't it?"

"You don't kiss and tell then?" Nathan joked.

Rachel made a zipping motion over her lips.

"When you two love birds have finished making eyes at each other," Kate cut in, "these are the people you'll be interviewing, DC Arthur."

"She's got the measure of us, it seems." Rachel said to Nathan as she took the file from Kate and opened it.

"Smart as a tack, this one," Nathan commented.

"I'm pretty sure that's sharp as a tack, actually," Kate corrected him.

"See what I mean?" Nathan said.

"She'll go far, with pedantry like that," Rachel agreed.

Kate rolled her eyes. "Piss off yeh twats."

Rachel laughed. "So, which lucky souls get to enjoy my scintillating conversational skills?"

"You're interviewing Chris Hewitt and Darcy Bain. They're employed at the Estate Agency that Jordan, our victim, owned. You've also got the two customers who were in the office that morning. We'll do the rest."

"Wilco, mon capi-tan," Rachel said with a grin. "I'll head off now and keep you updated with anything relevant."

"Great, thanks," Nathan replied as Rachel strode off. He turned to Kate. "Shall we get going?"

***

"What?!" Kay said as she pulled open the door nearly thirty seconds after Kate had rung the doorbell, holding a phone to her ear. Her hair was dishevelled, and her clothing wasn't much better. It was quite a departure from her slick, professional appearance when Kate had seen her in the office.

She looked stressed.

"Oh, sorry. I didn't realise…" she apologised upon recognising them and seeing their warrant cards. "Um, come in," she said, leading them inside. "Yeah, sorry, they're here now. Thanks. Bye," Kay said, ending the call.

Kate glanced at Nathan, who pulled a face at her that told her he thought Kay's appearance and demeanour were surprising. Kate bobbed her eyebrows and followed Kay inside. Noticing spotless cream carpets, Kate took a moment to give her shoes a proper shuffle on the mat and then decided to take them off anyway.

Kay smiled, apparently pleased with Kate's choice. Nathan did the same behind her with a grunt of annoyance.

"Everything okay, Mrs Seward?" Kate asked as she followed Kay into her living room. Kate took a seat on the sofa, finding a gap amidst the throw cushions that took up almost the whole thing. Nathan did the same with another muttered grumble.

"I'm fine," Kay answered, perching on the edge of a seat opposite them and dropping her head into her hands. "Just a little stressed is all. Trying to run this business on my own from home isn't easy. Made even harder by idiots leaving grotesque photos on my doorstep."

"Sorry, what?" Kate asked.

Kay picked up an envelope from the coffee table and handed it to Nathan. "It's what I was on the phone about. I just called the police about it when you two turned up."

Kate felt Nathan nudge her with his elbow. She glanced down to see him pulling the envelope open. Inside was another Polaroid, again showing Mark Summers looking beaten and starved. Below that, written on the white border, was a number and a word.

2 Days.

Kate nodded in acknowledgement and looked back to Kay. "This arrived today, did it?"

"I found it on my doorstep, not ten, fifteen minutes ago. I'd not stepped outside before then, so it could have been there all night."

"Do you have any cameras or did you hear anything?" Nathan asked, being careful about how he handled the envelope.

"No, nothing like that. The first I knew about it was when I opened the front door this morning. Does this have anything to do with Jordan?"

"Um, we're not sure yet, investigations are ongoing, and I can't talk about things in any great detail. What about the man in the photograph. Do you recognise him?"

Kay shook her head. "No, sorry. Should I?"

"No. Don't worry about it."

"Is it from the killer? Has he been here, on my property?" Kay asked, her voice rising in pitch as the idea took root. "Am I next?"

"Please, try not to worry. We'll look at getting a uniformed officer placed outside your house for a day or so. Would that help?"

Kay nodded, her fears mollified for the time being. "Oh my, I can't quite believe he's gone. After all these years, it's utter madness. I mean, who would want to kill him? Look, I'm sorry. It's just that I've been there from the beginning when he first set it all up. I'm really not sure what we're going to do, you know?"

Kate offered a consolatory smile. "I understand. May we ask you a few questions?"

"Of course. Sorry. Didn't mean to burden you with my problems. What do you need to know?"

"Your full name is Kay Evelyn Seward and you're married with two children?"

"That's right. They're older though, they've moved out."

"Okay. And you've been working at the Donaldson's Estate Agency for eight years?"

"From day one." She smiled to herself. "Those were the best days when it was just the two of us. No politics, just the dream of a successful business."

"So, did you know Jordan was working late the night he was murdered?"

Kay nodded. "Yes, I knew about it. He's something of a workaholic. Always putting in extra hours and making sure everything got done when it needed to. The success of the business is mainly down to him, you know."

"Were you aware that Naomi Sawyer was coming in to work with him?"

"No. But plenty of us do help out. He's very fair about it and makes sure we get paid overtime."

"So, it's not unusual for him to do that?"

"Not really, no."

"Were you aware of Jordan having any kind of relationship with Naomi?"

"Nothing beyond a typical working relationship, no. Jordan was a professional businessman and a kind, gentle person. He would never do anything to hurt Jo."

"You mean Joanna, his wife?"

"She's pregnant, you know. He'd never cheat on her in her condition."

"We understand," Nathan cut in. "We're just trying to get a sense of who he was and his relationships. Most murder victims are killed by people they know, usually family or friends, so we need to be sure."

"I understand, but I don't like his name being dragged through the mud. Jordan was a good man."

"Of course," Nathan answered.

"So where were you on the night in question?" Kate asked.

"I was here, at home with my husband. We were in all night," Kay answered.

"We'll need to speak to your husband, you understand?"

"Of course, he'll be back later."

Kate nodded. "We'll send someone over to take a statement from him."

Kay nodded with a sigh. "That's fine. So, when do you think we'll be able to get back into the office?"

CHAPTER 10

"By the looks of things, you were right to assume the earlier deadline," Kate said as they approached the building ahead on foot. "Now, it's just two days."

Nathan gave her a troubled look.

"He, or she, I guess, is taunting us," Kate said.

"Or they," Nathan added.

"Or they," Kate agreed. "But why send it to Kay? Does that mean she's next?"

"I don't know. I'm not sure what this guy's game is yet. The taunting messages are not uncommon for a serial killer, though. Anyway, she'll have an officer at her house for the next few days, so hopefully, that will set her mind at ease and deter the killer."

Kate nodded as they reached the door and pressed the buzzer beside a label with the name Hunter West written on it.

"Hello?" said a voice over the intercom.

"Hunter West?" Kate asked.

"That's right," the man replied.

"It's the Police, we're here to talk to you about Jordan Donaldson."

"Oh, okay, come on up," Hunter replied. The intercom clicked off as the lock on the door buzzed open. Kate led the way in with Nathan right behind her. Hunter lived in the upstairs flat in a large detached house, and as they walked into the downstairs hallway and looked up the stairs directly in front of them, Hunter stepped out of his front door and gave them a weak smile.

Kate smiled back and led the way up the carpeted steps. The décor was very dated and had seen better days, but she'd been in worse places.

As she approached the top, she looked up to see Hunter watching her. His eyes flicked up from further down her body, but he showed no signs of embarrassment for having been caught checking her out.

Kate showed him her warrant card on reaching the top of the stairs. "I'm DC O'Connell, and this is DS Halliwell. May we come in?"

"Of course." He moved back into his place and allowed her and Nathan inside with a brief greeting as they passed him.

Kate found herself in a kitchen-diner that appeared to stretch to the back of the house, and stood in stark contrast to the look of the hallway outside.

The place was well maintained with clean, modern décor and a very minimalist look to it. She felt surprised and actually quite impressed. It was clearly some kind of bachelor pad though, with the framed movie posters on the walls and the gaming controllers on the coffee table.

Apart from possibly needing a woman's touch, it was nice.

"Can I get you a drink? A coffee maybe?" Hunter asked.

"No, thanks," Kate replied.

"I'll pass," Nathan added.

Hunter shrugged. "Suit yourselves. I was wondering when you might come to visit."

"We're making our rounds, Mr West," Kate replied.

"Please, sit," Hunter said, gesturing to the sofa as he took a seat. Kate noticed he was looking at her much more than at Nathan, and felt like he was undressing her with his mind.

"And please, call me Hunter," he continued, giving her a more suggestive one-sided smile.

Kate took her seat beside Nathan and was already starting to get an idea of what kind of man Hunter was.

"I'd like to just confirm a few details, and then we have a few questions about the death of Jordan Donaldson, okay?"

"Fire away," he replied.

"Could you give me your full name, please?"

Hunter answered Kate's questions, confirming his identity and a few other details, without issue.

"So tell me about your relationship with Jordan Donaldson?"

"We're mates. I joined the business about five years ago. I didn't know him before then, but we became mates pretty quickly, really. A similar sense of humour maybe?"

"So, you're mates then?"

"Yeah. We're not shagging or anything."

Kate couldn't help the slight tick of confusion at his comment, but she let it slide.

"So tell me about your whereabouts on the night of Jordan's death, on the seventh," Kate asked.

"I was with some other mates at the pub. A few of us came back here for some Fifa, and then I hit the sack."

"Fifa?" Kate asked, the reference passing her by.

Hunter picked up a controller on the table and waved it at her. "Fifa 2018. Football game."

"I see. Okay. And your friends will confirm that for us, will they?"

"Yep."

"Can I have their details please?"

Hunter nodded and gave her a few names and numbers which they would chase up later. "They'll get a kick out of knowing I gave their numbers to a pretty cop."

Kate finished scribbling in her pad and looked up, an eyebrow raised. "Will they?" she answered, her tone flat.

"Are you single?" he asked.

"Mr West, that is none of your business, and I would ask that you stick to answering our questions and not getting sidetracked."

Hunter nodded. "Yeah, alright."

"So, how did Mr Donaldson seem to you in the days leading up to his death? Did you notice anything strange?"

"No, not really. He seemed quite normal to me."

"So, no strange behaviour? He didn't seem stressed or worried about anything?" Nathan added.

"No, nothing. He was fine."

"So, tell me about Naomi Sawyer," Kate asked.

"Naomi? Um, she's a work friend. Nice girl."

"Was Jordan close to her?"

"Oh. I see what you're getting at. Yeah, Jordan liked her. They'd known each other at school, I think. Before he met Joanna. Dated for a while back then."

"What about more recently?" Kate asked. "Did he say anything to you about them seeing each other?"

"We talked about her. You know, just guy stuff. He thought she was fit, and she is."

"And that was it? It was just talk? He never mentioned having an affair with her or anything?"

"Nah. We just talked."

"Would Jordan talk with anyone else in the office about her? What about Chris? Were they close?"

Hunter let out a short, loud laugh. "Hah! Nah, love. He wouldn't say anything to that queer."

"Excuse me," Kate answered, a little surprised at the turn of phrase.

"Chris is a woofter. He's gay."

"I'm aware of what queer means," Kate answered him, giving him an accusatory look. She didn't like his bigoted tone.

"Aaah, good. Well, no. He wouldn't talk to Chris. Chris hangs out with the girls more than with me or Jordan."

"Does he know Naomi well?"

"I don't think so. He chats with Robyn more than Naomi. And Kay."

"I see," Kate said. "And tell me about Robyn?"

"The weirdo? She's into that Voodoo shit. Witch stuff. Bit of a freak, if you ask me."

"So, you don't speak to her much?"

"Not if I can avoid it. I only talk to her for work stuff really."

"That's big of you," Kate muttered as she wrote in her pad. She wondered what Robyn's opinion of Hunter would be. Although she could probably guess.

"Do you have any information that might help us further on this investigation? Anything you've noticed or seen?" Nathan asked.

"I don't think so. It was a bit of a shock really when I heard. Just wondering if I have a job to go back to now."

"Well, if you do think of anything," Kate added, "here's the number of the station."

"Just the station?" he asked as they all rose from their seats. He looked at her, his expression questioning.

"Thank you for your time, Mr West," Kate said, and walked towards the door, aware that he was probably ogling her arse as she turned her back to him. She didn't care enough to say anything and led the way out after a quick acknowledgement of thanks to him.

He's a bit of a dick," Kate commented as they approached their car on the street outside.

"But did he do it?" Nathan asked.

"I don't think so," she answered as she climbed into the passenger side of the car. "I don't get that vibe from him at all. He's clearly an over-sexed man's man, looking to get his end away at the earliest opportunity, but as for a killer? No, my money's not on him. I don't think he did it."

"He didn't think much of Chris, though."

Kate shrugged. "Prejudice doesn't mean you're a killer."

"No, it doesn't. Well done, by the way. You handled him well. You've got good people skills. Do you want to lead the next two?"

Kate smiled, genuinely this time. "Sure, thanks. I'll give it a go."

"So, who's next on the list?"

Kate checked her notebook and the name and address listed inside. "Wilson Hollins, the property owner."

CHAPTER 11

"Well, someone's done alright for themselves," Nathan commented as he pulled up onto the drive of the gated property.

Kate admired the large, beautiful house on the other side and nodded. The three-story home was huge, with well-maintained gardens on a road of houses that were similar, or even bigger still.

Surrey was an affluent area with lots of very wealthy people living in the county, but it still had its fair share of residents living on or below the poverty line. Clearly, that wasn't an issue on this road though.

Nathan pulled up next to an intercom just in front of the gate and pressed the button. Moments later, Kate heard a male voice ask who they were. Kate guessed it was Wilson. Nathan answered, and seconds later, the gates opened remotely, granting them entry into the bricked driveway with enough room for several cars. There was already two in here, but that still left ample room for them to turn the car around and park up.

"I always enjoy coming to houses like this and being reminded that I chose the wrong career," Nathan commented.

Kate smiled. "So, you're saying I should quit and retrain?"

"Depends if you like money or not."

"Good point, I'll have to ponder that one. Hmmm, do I like money? Let me think..."

"Alright, little miss sarcastic, let's go chat with the millionaire," he said and climbed out the car.

Kate followed. "I bet he has good coffee."

"Oh, so you'll accept it off the rich man in the large house. Gotcha."

"Provided he doesn't ogle my tits."

"Because standards," Nathan answered as they approached the front door.

"Every girl's gotta have them. Shall I take the lead on this one too?"

"Go for it. You've got a good way with people."

"Unlike you?" Kate asked.

"Like you say, it's probably the tits."

"Get some implants, Mr Happy."

"I'm the grumpy one, haven't you noticed that yet?"

"I'm blocking it out, it's the only way I can stand to be around you."

Nathan smiled and shook his head as Kate pressed the doorbell. Moments later the large wooden door swung inwards revealing the shortish man with a shaved-bald head that they'd met at the office yesterday.

"Detectives. Welcome. Please, come in... Ooof," he said, as a little girl ran up behind him and grabbed his legs in a hug. She peered around them, her large eyes looking up at Kate with a mixture of curiosity and fear.

Kate smiled at the little girl. "Hi there. I'm Kate, and I'm a Policewoman."

The little girl backed up. "Police?"

"Yeah. Don't worry, we're not here to arrest anyone," Kate continued.

The girl looked out into the driveway and then back up at Nathan and Kate.

"Where's your police car?"

Kate smiled. "That's our police car out there. It's a secret one."

The girl looked up at her in wonder. "So you can sneak up on robbers?"

"That's right. We sneak up on them and grab them," Kate answered, making claws with her hands and reaching for her, but deliberately missing.

"Wow," the girl said, laughing.

"Shall we let the nice police people in now, Daisy? They want to speak to daddy."

"Okay," Daisy said, allowing her father to back up and let them in.

"Please, go through there and take a seat." He said to them. "I'll get Daisy settled in the playroom and be right back."

Kate nodded and smiled.

"Thanks, Mr Hollins," Nathan said and went into the front room on their right. It was large and like everything else they could see, clean and filled with expensive-looking furniture and ornaments.

Kate caught Nathan's eye and whispered to him. "Playroom? La-di-da."

"Like I said, wrong job."

Neither of them sat on the seats spread around the space they walked into. Instead, Kate made a slow circuit of the room, running her eyes over the photos and items on display. Nathan also took an interest in the pictures, but was less subtle about it, just walking right up to them and squinting at them.

Kate heard the sound of the television going on in another room and made her way back towards the sofa with a quick hiss at Nathan to join her.

He glanced back at her but didn't rush over. Instead, he took his time and finished his perusal of the photos on the cabinet, looking up as Wilson strode back into the room.

"Sorry to keep you, officers. Please, take a seat. How can I help you? I take it this is about Jordan Donaldson."

"That's right," Kate replied, sitting on the sofa. Nathan walked over and joined her, as she checked Wilson's full name and some other basic details.

"So you were at the office, the morning after the night of the murder," Kate began.

"That's right. I had a meeting with Jordan that morning. It had been in the diary a while. I parked up behind the office as usual. Jordan's car was there, so when I learned he wasn't in, I figured he'd gone out to get a coffee or something," he said with a shrug. That's when you guys turned up."

"Okay. I see. And what about the night of the murder? Were you home?"

"I worked late that night at my office. My secretary was there. She'll confirm where I was."

"I see, and what time were you there until?"

"Oh, around ten, ten-thirty, maybe? I was home shortly after that. Caught my wife before she went to bed. Watched a little TV and joined her a little later on."

"So, you say your secretary can confirm you were at your office on the night in question?"

"That's right. Her name is Stacy Lee. Would you like to speak to her?"

"We would," Kate confirmed, and Wilson gave her his secretary's phone number.

"I must say, I'm shocked that something like this should happen to an upstanding member of the community like Jordan. He's a great guy. I mean, why would someone do this to someone like him?"

"Well, that's what we're trying to find out, Mr Hollins."

"Of course, of course."

"Did you know Jordan well?"

"Only on a professional basis. We saw each other most months as I like to keep an eye on my units and properties, but that was all. My wife knows Joanna a little better, though. They've had coffee a few times."

"I see. We might need to speak to her as well then."

"I'm sure that can be arranged. She's out right now, but I'll let her know you want to talk."

"Thank you. We'll be in touch soon, later today perhaps, to arrange taking her statement."

"Were you aware of any problems surrounding Jordan? Any relationships within the business that might have led to this?"

"I'm sorry, no. I'm not there very often and don't take much interest in the relationships of the workers."

"Understandable," Nathan said.

"No. He paid his bills on time, looked after the property, and was always kind and polite to me. A model tenant, really."

"Do you know any of the other workers well?" Kate asked.

"Not well, no. I know them to say hi to, but that's all. They seem nice."

"So, I understand from our search of the unit, there's no security cameras in the office?" Nathan asked.

"It's on the list to have fitted, but Donaldson's isn't a shop with goods that can be pilfered, so it just got delayed. Besides, there are the cameras on the street outside. It wasn't something that Jordan was pushing me for. It would have been disruptive for his business anyway."

"Having the CEO murdered is probably more disruptive," Kate interjected, disliking his reply.

"We know about the cameras outside. That's not as helpful as having a camera inside though, is it?" Nathan continued.

"Yeah. I understand. I do regret that now. Jordan was a good man. This should never have happened to him."

"No, it shouldn't. But you're sat here nice and safe in your ivory tower, right?" Kate replied. She disliked the corporate greed and indifference of the rich that she saw all too often these days. But when it led, directly or not, to the death of an innocent man, she found it difficult not to say something.

Wilson glanced up at her, his expression unreadable, but then he nodded. "You're right. I wish I'd done more. It won't change what's happened, but I'll make sure Mrs Donaldson has everything she needs."

Kate's anger lessened a fraction as she listened to him and found herself unable to form a reply. So, she just nodded.

"Okay," Nathan said, getting up from the sofa. "Thank you Mr Hollins, you've been most helpful. I think we have what we need. We'll be in touch if we need anything further."

"Thank you," Kate said, pressing her lips together in a thin smile, before following Nathan from the house and back to the car.

He was looking a little frustrated as he slumped into the driver's seat. "Standing up against our corporate overlords in there, were you?"

"Sorry. They just annoy me sometimes."

"Yeah, me too," Nathan admitted.

"Do you think he's guilty?"

"Of corporate negligence, maybe. There really should be working cameras in that office, but as usual, it's too expensive and disruptive to implement, which makes our job all the more difficult." He sighed, sagging into his seat.

"Everything okay?" Kate asked.

"Dead ends. Everywhere we look is just a dead end right now. We need to catch a break."

"So, you don't think it was a co-worker that did it?"

"Not any of these, no. The people with the strongest motives so far are his wife, and maybe Naomi, if she really was having an affair with him."

"Well, we have one more person to visit and I, for one, am interested in what she has to say."

"Robyn?"

"The girl with the pentagram around her neck, yes."

"Alright. Let's go see what she has to say for herself."

CHAPTER 12

"Rachel's going to get a statement from Stacey Lee," Nathan said, stuffing his phone into his trouser pocket as they walked up through the block of flats and along the balcony corridor to the front door of the address Kate was double-checking on her phone.

"Here we are, number thirty-six," she said, returning her phone to her inside jacket pocket and removing her warrant card as she knocked.

The door jerked open a few inches, a steel chain stopping it from opening any further as a face appeared in the gap. The girl's face looked Kate up and down. "Yes?"

"Robyn Boyce?" Kate asked.

"Who's askin'?"

Kate held up her identification. "DC O'Connell and this is DS Halliwell. We'd like to come in and ask you a few questions, please."

Robyn eyed the badge for a moment, and then glanced between Kate and Nathan. Kate smiled back. Robyn pursed her lips and then rolled her eyes.

"Alright, one second," she said with an exasperated sigh. The door shut and Kate could hear the chain being removed before it opened again. "Come in, shut the door behind you."

"Thanks," Kate said, walking into the small flat and getting a strong whiff of marijuana. The flat consisted of one main room with a small double bed, some sofas, an attached kitchenette, and a single door to another room that Kate guessed would be the bathroom.

It was a little dark in here. The nets on the windows and the half-open curtains cast the corners of the room into shadow. Posters of heavy metal bands covered the walls, and the whole place looked like it could do with a clean-up. There weren't any used food cartons or dirty plates out, but there was an abundance of crap all around the place. Books and magazines piled up on the floor and table. DVD and Blu Ray cases, video game cases, bills and other letters left in messy piles. Admittedly, there wasn't much room in the whole flat by the looks of things, but a little work to get rid of some of the rubbish would likely go a long way.

"Sorry to bother you at home," Kate said as she took in the environment that Robyn lived in.

"Whatever," Robyn answered dropping onto the sofa.

Robyn didn't look pleased to have two detectives invading her home, and sat with her chin propped up on her fist, staring into the middle distance. Kate frowned and glanced at Nathan, who shrugged.

There was only one sofa in here. Kate looked around for another seat but couldn't see one. But she did spot a Japanese sword on a black wooden stand on a shelf on the far wall.

Kate stared at it for a long moment as images from her past rose up from the depths of her memory. Images from her teenage years, just after the death of her aunt.

She remembered walking through a house that was in a much worse state than this flat, with dirty plates and empty takeaway cartons everywhere. She clearly remembered spotting the same style of sword on the fireplace in that house in Cork, and what it possibly had signified back then.

She also remembered being discovered by a resident she hadn't realised was in the building when she'd snuck in, and then being chased from the house.

Kate took a deep breath to calm her nerves as she looked back at Robyn.

"So, we just need to confirm a few things first," she said, making her way through some basic questions about Robyn and her life, including details about the boyfriend she lived with.

"We have a few questions regarding the death of Jordan Donaldson, and your movements on the night of his murder."

Robyn nodded, taking her chin off her hand and looking up. "Sure."

"Can you confirm your whereabouts on the evening of Jordan's murder?"

"I was here."

"And can anyone confirm that?"

"My boyfriend," Robyn replied.

"That's Patrick Norman, right? And where is he?"

"That's right. He's at work," she answered, her voice sounding fed up already.

"And where does he work?"

"At Riverstone's Bookshop in town. He'll be there all day."

"We're going to need to speak to Patrick," Kate said.

Robyn sighed, clearly exasperated. "Sure. Why not?"

"So you've worked for Jordan for a little under a year, correct?" Kate asked.

"That's right," Robyn answered.

"And how're you finding it?"

"S'alright, I guess."

"You guess?"

"It's a job, innit?"

"I guess so," Kate replied.

"Have you noticed anything strange recently? Especially anything to do with Jordan?"

"Like what?"

"Anything. Any jealousy? Bad feeling? Anyone been coming to the office upset with him?"

Robyn shrugged. "No, nothin' like that."

"Okay, good," Kate answered, noting that it fit with what everyone else had been saying so far.

"What about any relationships in the office? Did you see Jordan getting close to anybody...?" Nathan asked.

Robyn sighed. "Alright, yeah. I did see Jordan kissing Naomi once."

Kate flinched and raised her eyebrows. "You saw them kissing?"

"I don't think I was meant to," Robyn added.

"Okay. And did they see you?"

"No. They didn't."

"And did you tell anyone about this?" Nathan asked.

"Only Norm."

"Norm?"

"My boyfriend," Robyn explained.

"And that's it?" Kate asked.

Robyn nodded.

"Tell me about your relationships with everyone in the office. Do you get on with everyone?"

"With most of them, I guess."

"So, not all of them?"

"Hunter's a dick, Naomi's a prissy cow, but Kay's okay, and so is Chris."

"You don't like Hunter, then?"

"That's what I just said, innit?"

Kate bit her lip to keep from answering her back. "It's important we know about all the relationships in the office, in case they have any influence on this case, so I was just trying to clarify your statement."

"Sure, let me make it clearer for you. He's a fuckin' dick. Thinks he's better than everyone else and he makes it clear how much he dislikes me. Okay?"

"So, he bullies you?" Kate asked, interested.

"I guess," Robyn answered, suddenly dismissive after her outburst.

"What about Jordan? Does he know about this?"

Robyn sighed. "Yeah, he knew."

"You told him?"

"He's seen it happen. He didn't stop it. He laughed at it once. I complained to him a while back, but he didn't do anything about it."

"So he joins in with Hunter?"

"I don't think he sees the harm. I think he sees it as office banter, but..."

"...but it's not." Kate finished for her and wrote *'motive'* in her notepad.

Robyn shook her head. "I hate him sometimes."

"Who? Hunter or Jordan?"

"Take your pick," Robyn answered.

"Have you spoken to anyone about this? Kay Seward, maybe?" Kate asked.

"What difference would that make? Anyway, he's dead now."

"Does Patrick know?"

Robyn nodded. "I told him. He got angry about it, but what can we do?"

"I understand," Kate answered, and glanced at the sword on the shelf, running through the evidence in her mind. There were occult influences everywhere. There was a reason for her and Patrick to hate Jordan, and there was an interest in dangerous weapons.

"I see you like your heavy metal," Nathan cut in.

"Yeah, so what?" Robyn answered, clearly unhappy with this new line of questioning before it had even really begun.

"You're into the occult too? I see you're wearing the same pentagram necklace I saw on you yesterday," Kate added.

"What's that got to do with anything?"

"Just answer the question please," Nathan barked.

"Yeah, I'm into Wicca and Paganism a bit. So what?"

"What about Satanism?" Kate asked, keen to drill into this a little more as memories of her aunt's murder and its parallels with this case swam to the forefront of her mind.

"What? No. That would require me to believe in Christianity, which I don't."

"You don't?"

"No. I'm not some crazy Satanist. Wicca is about living in harmony with your environment. We praise life and spirit and believe in helping people."

Kate nodded but didn't answer. It wasn't what she'd been expecting, but her suspicion wasn't on Robyn.

"Whose sword is that?" Nathan asked.

Kate looked up and caught Nathan glancing at her with a quick wink.

"That's my boyfriend's. That's not mine."

"Is he a martial artist?" Nathan pressed.

"No. He just likes it, I guess."

Does he? Kate thought, adding that to the strikes against Patrick's name.

"He needs to be careful with that. Don't go walking around outside with it."

"As if. We're not morons you know," Robyn answered him as Kate stepped away and looked around. Approaching the kitchen, she spotted a curious shape tucked into a corner on the counter and moved to get a better look.

It was a bong. Kate raised an eyebrow and turned back to Robyn. "Do you use drugs often?"

"Not really," Robyn answered.

"It stinks of marijuana in here," Nathan stated.

"Flavoured incense," Robyn replied with a grin, pointing to the pot on the table with several incense sticks inside it.

"But you've smoked it?" Kate asked.

Robyn sighed. "Alright, yes. I've had some before. Is that what you want to hear?"

"Have you tried anything else?"

"Don't remember," Robyn answered.

Kate sighed.

"Alright, I think we've heard enough," Nathan said. "Kate?"

"Yeah, I agree," Kate said, looking down at her notes and the clear suspicion it placed squarely on the shoulders of Robyn's boyfriend. "We'll be in touch, Miss Boyce," she said, checking the time and wondering how quickly they could get into town.

She had some pointed questions to ask Patrick Norman.

Leaving the flat, Kate dropped into the passenger seat and looked over at Nathan. "Did you reach the same conclusion as me?"

"You think Patrick Norman did it?"

"And you don't?" Kate asked incredulously.

"I don't know, something doesn't fit here," Nathan replied, frowning in concentration.

"What? What do you mean? We have Robyn clearly being bullied by Hunter and Jordan. She told her boyfriend who's a drug user and clearly has an interest in the occult and bladed weapons. What doesn't fit?"

"I don't know. It's just not what I thought…" Nathan explained.

"Not what you thought? Did you think something else was going on?"

"I don't know. Maybe?"

"Is this the conspiracy stuff the other detectives warned me about?" she asked, getting a clearer idea of how his views might taint the investigation.

"So, they spoke to you then?"

"Briefly."

Nathan sighed. "No, you're right. It all fits. We definitely need to speak with Patrick Norman."

"Good," Kate said, feeling her trust in Nathan, built up through the events of the past day and a half, crumble just a little bit. Was DI Sam Mason right about Nathan? Would he potentially ruin her career if he followed his prejudices? She'd need to keep an eye on things better.

"Where did she say he worked?"

CHAPTER 13

As Nathan placed a Police Identification Card in the window of their unmarked car—in case any parking wardens got any ideas—Kate climbed out onto the pedestrianised road in central Guildford. They were less than ten metres from the front of Riverstone's Bookshop, but didn't want to park right outside of it.

"Alright, do you think he's in there?" Kate asked. The drive over had been a quiet one, with the only meaningful conversation being their call to dispatch to inform them of their plan of action.

They wanted to bring Patrick in and ask him a few questions.

"Let's hope so," Nathan said, sounding a little brighter. "You're good at this, you know. You'll go far."

Kate felt her smile grow and a flush of heat in her cheeks. "Shut it, you'll make my head swell."

"At least then I'll be able to get through the door before you and make the arrest."

"Steal my glory? I don't think so," she answered him as they walked in the entrance of the shop. It was busy, there were shoppers everywhere, and after a quick sweep around, it wasn't clear where Patrick Norman might be. The shop was deep with several floors, and that wasn't counting the staff areas out back. He could be anywhere.

"What do you think?" Kate asked.

"Let's speak to the girl on the till. See if she knows where he is."

Kate nodded and followed Nathan over to the side of the counter, where the young woman was serving people.

"Miss?" Nathan said, holding his warrant card where she could clearly see it. Kate did the same. "Do you have a second?"

The girl looked at the identification cards, a look of surprise crossing her face. "Um, sure," she said and handed some change to the customer she'd been serving before telling the next one to wait a moment. "What's up?"

"We're looking for one of your colleagues, Patrick Norman," Nathan said.

"Pat?"

"That's right. Do you know where he is?"

"Yeah, he's over..." she began, craning her neck to look back towards the front entrance. Kate turned to see a young man holding some books stand up from where he'd been crouched, stacking shelves. He wore the same polo shirt as the girl with the shop's logo on his chest and stood staring at them. He was tall, thin, with longish dyed-black hair, and a nose ring and he was staring at Kate's warrant card which was clearly in view still.

"Oh, he's right there," the cashier said, pointing to the young man with the shocked expression.

Patrick glanced between Kate and Nathan for a heartbeat.

"Patrick?" Nathan began.

He turned and ran.

Patrick sprinted through the front of the shop. Dropping his books, he knocked a few people out of the way in his bid to make the high street, and freedom.

"Goddammit," Nathan cursed as Kate bolted after Patrick with Nathan hot on her heels. She threaded her way through the shop, shouting, "Police. Move," as she went.

Within seconds she was out on the high street and turning left to follow Patrick up the road.

The high street sloped upwards, and she could clearly see Patrick a short distance ahead, his arms pumping as he ran up the hill as fast as he could. Kate focused on putting one foot in front of the other and kept her breathing even to avoid getting a stitch as she ran after him. The cobblestone road was uneven underfoot, and she was glad she wasn't wearing anything with a bigger heel.

"Patrick, stop. We just want to talk," she yelled after him as people dodged sideways to get out of the way. She glanced back to see Nathan still behind her, but he looked like he was flagging quicker than she was.

She'd probably have to apprehend this one herself.

As Patrick neared the Guildhall on the left of the high street, with its iconic black and gold clock projected out over the pedestrians below, he veered right. Opposite the Guildhall was Tunsgate Arch, an ornate building with pillars that served as the entrance onto Tunsgate Road.

He'd probably had enough of running up a hill, and this would be his route off of it.

She shouted at him again. "Police, stop!"

She could see that the hill had taken a toll on Patrick. He was moving at a much slower rate than he had been initially, as he made for the steps up into the archway. Forcing herself on, her thighs and calves burning from the run, Kate closed the gap.

Patrick misjudged the steps in his exhaustion, tripped over the top step, and stumbled, falling face-first on the ground.

Kate was only metres behind him and leapt up the four steps in a single bound just as Patrick was getting back to his feet. She pushed him back down and sat on him, gasping for breath.

"Gimmie your hands," she ordered him, her voice breathless as she pulled her cuffs from the harness under her jacket.

"Patrick Norman, I am arresting you on suspicion of murder. You do not have to say anything. But it may harm your defence if you do not mention when questioned, something which you later rely on in court. Anything you do say may be given in evidence. Do you understand?"

The cuffs made that satisfying clicking noise as she secured his hands, but Patrick didn't answer.

"Taking a breather are we, O'Connell?"

Kate looked up from where she'd basically sat on Patrick's back and raised an eyebrow. "Shut it old man. At least I caught him."

Nathan offered her his hand. "Up you get. Suspects are not furniture."

"Ugh. But I was comfy," she grunted as she got back to her feet. Her legs felt like jelly, so she moved to a nearby pillar and leant against it while Nathan pulled Patrick back to his feet. Around them, people had stopped to watch the arrest, with several of them filming it. With a sigh, Kate got her game face on and stepped away from the pillar.

"Go about your day, everyone. Move along. This is police business," she said as she took hold of Patrick's other arm and guided him back to their car.

They'd take him back to Horsley Station and get him booked in. Kate was looking forward to their forthcoming chat.

CHAPTER 14

"She didn't do it," Nathan said, sitting at his desk back at the station.

"How can you be so sure?" Kate asked.

"Robyn's young and into the whole goth scene. That doesn't make her a killer," Nathan explained.

"And our friend downstairs?"

"Now, I think he's a more likely candidate, but I'm still not convinced. The evidence is compelling, but I'm not sure it sits right with me yet."

"I suppose Robyn's statement of being home with him casts doubt on our theory," Kate challenged him. "Unless they were in on it together?"

"I don't know. I'm not sure I can see her committing murder of the kind we saw out there the other day."

"So where do you think the suspicion lies?"

"As far as motive, Patrick's is strong, but I'm not sure it's enough to take things to the level of killing someone. Also, it sounds like Hunter was the main bully, not Jordan."

"But Jordan ignored Robyn's complaint and joined in."

Nathan shrugged. "To me, I think Joanna and Naomi's ex are stronger candidates."

"If Joanna knew about the rumoured affair," Kate added.

"True..."

"And if Steve is still on the scene with Naomi."

"Also true," Nathan admitted.

"That doesn't explain the sacrificial nature of the death though."

"I would guess that's something we don't know about yet."

"Also, if it was Joanna, how on earth did she manage to string Jordan up to a tree? Would she be strong enough?"

"Maybe she had help."

Kate smiled, noting the similarity to her idea that Robyn and Patrick were in on it together. "Touché."

"We'll see where it goes. I have people out looking for Steve, trying to track him down," Nathan said, looking up as Rachel walked over to join them, stopping beside the big board.

"How'd it go?" Nathan asked.

"Nothing much to write home about, really. Chris and Darcy both have solid alibis for the time of death. Chris said he didn't really get on well with Hunter West, but other than that, both of them seemed to get along with everyone in the office for the most part."

"Hunter made his opinions about Chris' love life clear to us as well," Kate said.

"Oh, really?"

"Yeah, a bit of a dick by all accounts," Kate answered.

"And the customers?" Nathan asked.

"Same. Good alibis and no motive," Rachel said.

"I've got some of the investigators looking into the company's client history," Nathan added. "Just in case there's a former customer that's come back for revenge."

"Sounds like a long shot," Kate commented.

"In all likelihood. But we need to make sure we cover all options here," Nathan explained. "What about Stacy Lee?"

"I spoke with her," Rachel answered. "She confirms Wilson's story that he was with her at the office that night."

"More office romance?" Kate wondered out loud.

Rachel shrugged. "Just sounds like everyone's getting it more than I am."

"I'm sure DI Burnham would be happy to help with that," Nathan commented.

"Oh, yuck. No thanks. I'd rather be celibate," Rachel replied.

Nathan laughed. "Alright, thank you, Rachel. I'll let you know if we need you again."

Rachel moved off back to her desk as Kate settled into her chair and logged in.

"Autopsy report is in," Nathan said over his shoulder, just as she spotted the notification on her screen.

"I see it," she said, opening it up. She spent the next few minutes reading through it and making sure she understood what it was telling her.

"That's mostly as we had guessed," Nathan commented.

Kate nodded as she read through the conclusion again. It appeared that Jordan had been tortured while still alive and killed by the stab wound to the heart, which was nothing new, but Toxicology revealed traces of Ketamine in his system, which was likely used to keep him sedated for transportation.

"So, the killer choked Jordan to knock him out, pumped him full of Ketamine to keep him under, and transported him to the woods where he strung him up and tortured him to death," Nathan summarised.

There was nothing found on Jordan that could lead to identifying the killer though, Kate noted with a little frustration.

"Ketamine. It's used recreationally too," Kate suggested. "I wonder if Patrick has used it before?"

"Well, let's go find out, shall we?"

***

"Where were you on the night of the seventh?" Kate asked.

Patrick sat across the table from her and Nathan, head down, looking sullen, and thoroughly unhappy to be there. Beside him, the duty solicitor who had been assigned to Patrick took notes.

"I've told you, I was at home with Robyn."

"Doing what? Kate asked.

"I don't know."

"You don't know what you were doing?"

"Just the usual, like. You know, watching TV, playing Pub-G."

"Pub-G?"

"PlayStation game," he explained.

"Right. So, tell me about the sword?" Nathan asked.

"What about it?"

"Why do you have it?"

"Cos it looks nice. Not illegal, is it?" Patrick challenged him.

"Why did you run from us?" Kate asked.

"I don't know. I panicked. I thought it might be about the drugs I've taken..."

"Do you take drugs often?" Kate pressed.

"Only when I'm stressed."

"Like today?" Nathan asked.

Patrick shrugged.

"What about Ketamine? Have you ever used Ketamine, Patrick?" Kate continued.

"Once or twice. I prefer weed, though."

"But you have used it?"

"Ages ago. Why?"

"Tell me about your interest in the occult," Kate said.

"Really?"

"You *are* interested in it, right?" Kate continued.

"I guess. It's cool."

"Are you a follower of Wicca?"

"Not really. Robyn is into that more than me," Patrick answered. "I'm an atheist. I don't believe in any religion."

"But you like the occult?" Nathan asked.

"What do you like? Football?" Patrick asked Nathan and then looked at Kate. "EastEnders? I like myth, fantasy, and the occult. So what? Look, where are you going with this? It all seems like a giant waste of time to me," He said, sitting back in his chair and folding his arms across his chest.

"How well do you know Jordan Donaldson?" Nathan asked.

Patrick's eyebrows shot up. "You think I killed him?" he asked, his voice incredulous.

"That's not what I asked," Nathan said.

Patrick sighed. "I don't, really. I've seen him a couple of times when I've dropped Robyn off to work, but that's it really. Don't know the dude."

"But you know he bullied your girlfriend."

"He was a bit rude to her a couple of times. Hunter is worse. They're idiots. I've told Robyn she can change jobs whenever she likes."

"Were you angry when you heard about the bullying?"

"A bit, I guess. Is that what you think might be my motive?" He laughed. "Pretty weak sauce, guys."

"But you were angry."

Patrick sighed. "For half an hour or so, months ago, maybe. Robyn's a big girl you know, she can handle herself."

"I'm not sure I believe you," Nathan said. "You're a drug user with an interest in blades and the occult, and your girlfriend was being bullied by the man who's currently lying dead in the morgue. A man who was killed with a blade in a ritualistic, occult fashion. You can see why I'm a little suspicious of you."

Patrick frowned and leant forward. "You can be suspicious all you like, but I didn't do it, and you can't prove that I did. Also, I have a witness that I was at home all night."

"Unless Robyn, the victim of the abuse, who also has a keen interest in the occult, was in on it with you."

Patrick laughed. "That's funny. In fact, hang on, there should be a record of us being online and active that night... Yeah. We were both logged into the PlayStation Network that night. There'll be a record of us being online."

"Is that right?" Nathan asked.

Kate sat back and pressed her lips together. If he was telling the truth, she knew he was right. She'd not indulged in much gaming in her life. It wasn't something she took a significant interest in, but she was aware enough to know that if they were playing online, there would likely be a record of that somewhere.

"Yeah, it is. In fact, I can check on my phone, I think. I can see when I was logged in on the website. Can I have my phone back, please? I'll show you."

***

Kate watched Nathan practically throw the file he was holding onto his desk as he walked up to it. She knew how he was feeling.

The records of Patrick's online gaming were about as solid an alibi as anyone was likely to have. They clearly showed he was online until the early hours on the night of the murder, and so was Robyn. With them backing up each other's stories, added to the possibility of them getting witness statements from the other people they'd been playing with online, it was crystal clear that Patrick and Robyn were almost certainly, not the killers.

"Looks like we're back to square one," Nathan muttered.

Kate nodded. "Yeah. Now what? It feels like a step backwards."

"Nathan sighed as he sat down. "You can't think of it like that. We've eliminated two possible suspects who we now know, are not the killers."

"I know. It just felt right, though. Everything seemed to fit."

Nathan shrugged. "And yet, it didn't." He turned to his desk as Kate took her seat and logged into her computer. The next hour was taken up with entering details in the system and passing reports around.

An hour after the interview, the system alerted her to a new piece of evidence that had just come in.

"Are you seeing this?" Nathan asked.

"Just looking now," Kate said and opened up the report. It detailed emails between Jordan and Naomi, through an account on Jordan's computer that was not affiliated with his work.

It didn't take much reading for her to find some of the juicier parts.

"Alright, well, I think that makes it abundantly clear that something was going on between Naomi and Jordan," Kate said as she read an email from Naomi describing what she was going to do to Jordan that night when they worked late.

"It certainly does. We'll have to read through these, but we should look at getting Naomi back in to answer some more questions."

"She'll have a hard time denying all this," Kate agreed, as she saw DI Mason wandering over.

"You know, I always enjoy my visits to this part of the office," he said.

"We sent you the report from today," Nathan said.

"I know. I read it. So, what was all that in Guildford town centre earlier on? Couldn't be a little more discreet perhaps?"

"He made a run for it; we couldn't let him get away."

DI Mason sighed. "Good thing you had Kate with you, otherwise he would have."

Kate caught Nathan's glance at her and then looked up at Sam. "Nathan was right behind me, he would have caught him part way up Tunsgate had the chase not ended when it did."

"Would he now?"

"He would," Kate replied, her voice full of confidence.

"And you've just let him go?"

"Despite good intelligence that led to our suspicions about him, he has a solid alibi backed up by multiple witnesses and evidence. He didn't do it," Kate replied.

"Alright. So you have some more leads?"

"We do, we'll follow them up tomorrow," Nathan answered.

"See that you do."

CHAPTER 15

He watched the counsellor enter the room and sit opposite him.

The older man took his time, settling himself into the chair, before looking up and meeting his eye. He was thin, wearing a long dark coat with a suit beneath. His hair was slicked back and greying, but there was an intelligence behind those eyes.

A great intelligence, as well as a feeling of threat. He was a dangerous man who'd seen much throughout his life.

"Doyen," he said in greeting to the counsellor.

The counsellor gave him a thin smile, but there was no joy in it at all. "Proselyte. We're worried. The council is worried. The Herald is concerned too. Your recent actions. They're a little concerning, a little too public."

"I have it under control," he reassured the councillor.

"Do you? You have the police after you after the mess you left in the woods. You know that, right?"

"The police do not concern me, and they should not concern you. I'm monitoring them, but compared to the great work, they're of little importance."

"Be aware, Proselyte, should things progress to the point where they pose a threat to us, we will take action."

He nodded once. He'd seen it happen before. The secrecy of the group outweighed everything else. Even the great works such as what he had embarked upon, were secondary to the group's secrecy.

He knew the cost of failure, and he would gladly accept the Chasm if he failed his self-appointed task.

"I will be careful, and I know the cost. You have nothing to fear from me. Preparations are progressing well, and I shall be ready for the second dedication shortly."

"I wish you luck, Proselyte. It's a lonely path you walk, but the Herald will reward you greatly should you succeed."

"Thank you, Doyen. I will not let you, the Herald, or The Hand down."

"See that you don't."

CHAPTER 16

Kate woke with a yell, as fear gripped her. She sat up in bed, breathing hard, her skin wet with sweat as she stared into the shadows of her apartment.

It was the usual nightmare.

She was alone, in Ireland, hunting for her aunt's killer. She'd been convinced about who it was and had finally confronted him late one night in a car park. Her mind had been filled with the usual flashes of violence as the man attacked her.

In some of the dreams, she fought back, in others, she was the victim, and suddenly the man was standing over her in the same stone circle that Fiona had been killed in, a knife in his hand.

But that man, Duane, hadn't been the killer. She'd been wrong.

But this time, it hadn't been Duane attacking her, this time it was Patrick.

She'd been in the car park, waiting, when Patrick walked out of the shadows carrying his samurai sword. He'd gloated about being the real killer before swinging the blade.

That's when she'd woken up.

She wiped her forehead as her breathing slowed. As she calmed down, her eyes looked over to the bookcase, and the cardboard folder sitting on the shelf between her other books.

It was at times like this when the contents of that folder weighed heavily on her mind. But there was nothing she could do.

With a sigh, she dropped back into the soft, welcoming embrace of her pillow, and pulled the duvet tight around her as she went back to sleep.

She didn't see or hear the envelope being pushed under her door as she drifted back to sleep.

***

Kate walked right up to Nathan's desk and stood over him, holding up the plastic sandwich bag before her. Nathan looked up and took a second to focus on the bag with the envelope inside it.

He frowned. "He didn't…"

Kate nodded. "Oh, he did. Found it this morning, pushed under the door to my flat. He knows where I live."

"Shit. Have you opened it?"

"Once, carefully, with gloves on. It's the same thing. A photo of Mark, with '1 Day' written under it."

Nathan sighed. "Are you okay?"

Kate shrugged. "I'm a little shaken up, but I'll be fine," she answered, thinking back to the moment she opened the unmarked envelope and the feelings of fear and nausea that rose up within her as the realisation that the killer had been right outside her door, settled into her mind. The memories of visiting the stone circle as a teenager where her aunt had been killed came rushing back as well. She didn't get the feeling she was a target for this killer, though.

"Do you want someone placed outside your flat, like Kay?"

Kate smiled. "No, I don't think so..."

"Are you sure?"

"Don't worry about me. I think he's just showing off."

"Taunting us," Nathan added, mimicking her comment about him yesterday.

Kate nodded. "Something like that," she said and placed the bag on Nathan's desk. "I'll let you deal with that while I get myself settled," she said and went about getting herself a coffee and pulling open the reports and files on the system. She wasn't sure how long she'd been sat there, typing and cross-checking things when Nathan called her name from behind her.

"Hey, what's up?" Kate said, turning to look at him.

"Want to leave that paperwork for a bit and come look at some CCTV footage?" he asked, like a parent tempting their child with some sweets.

"Ugh! Do I ever. Get me away from this computer, please!" she answered.

Nathan smiled. "Over here."

Kate scooted her chair over to Nathan's desk, where a video was paused on his screen, showing the street outside Donaldson's Estate Agents at night.

"Alright, our team's been working all night going through footage from across town, as well as from outside the Estate Agents. Now, watch this," he said and clicked play. The speed was set slightly faster than real life, but it was clear what was going on. "See this car pulling in there?"

"Yeah. Who is that?"

"That, we're reasonably sure, is Joanna. The video isn't super clear, we've had it enhanced, but from what we can make out of the number on the plate, and the make and model of the car, it's extremely unlikely to be anyone else.

"This is the night of the murder?" Kate asked

"Correct. So Joanna was there, at the office that night."

"But she's still in the car."

"She is, and if we keep going... There, you see that?"

"The car?" Kate asked, watching another vehicle move into frame and drive in front of Joanna's car and through the gap between the buildings to the back of the shops.

"Guess whose car that is?"

"Naomi's?" Kate guessed.

"Correct. Which fits with her statement. She was there, and she drove right past Joanna. And there she goes," he said, as Joanna's car drove away.

"She saw Naomi, didn't she?"

"That's what I think. I think she saw Naomi pull up and drive around back."

"She was there to catch them. She wanted to see them or maybe confront them," Kate hypothesised. "So she either knew or suspected that they were having an affair and wanted to confirm it at the very least."

"Looks that way. I'm wondering why she left though."

"She'll have bottled it," Kate suggested. "Or maybe she planned to confront him later. So, how long was Naomi there for?"

"Hold on," Nathan said and checked something before jumping the video forward a stretch. "Here's Naomi leaving. We don't see her at all the whole time she's back there, and she's behind the office for twenty minutes."

"That's quite a while," Kate said, sitting back.

"Long enough to subdue someone, and drag them into the back of a car," Nathan said.

"Maybe..." Kate answered, unsure if she believed that Naomi was capable of that. "Either way, they both lied to us."

"That they did. So, we know that Jordan and Naomi were having an affair and that Joanna, at the very least, suspected something was going on. So much so, that she drove into town to catch them in the act," Nathan said, summarising the evidence.

"That's a strong motive right there," Kate said. "She knew that her husband was having an affair, or at least found out about it or suspected it that night, only for Jordan to be found dead the next day."

"It doesn't look good for her," Nathan added.

"Which she will know, which is probably why she lied."

"Covering her tracks."

"Exactly," Kate agreed. "But while Joanna has a motive, Naomi had the opportunity. I'm guessing there's no footage of the back of the shops?"

"Not that we can find, no," Nathan answered.

"So, we can't rule her out either. I'm not sure what Naomi's motive would be to kill him, but she was right there on the night of the murder."

"At the very least she might have seen something," Nathan suggested.

Kate nodded. "She might have. I have to say, I don't get the feeling that she would be a killer. She's slim and doesn't show any signs of working out either, so I'm not convinced she'd be able to move the body."

"Adrenaline is a powerful thing, though," Nathan countered.

Kate nodded in agreement.

"But I agree. I think Joanna is a more likely suspect. She has a much stronger and clearer motive and is much more invested in Jordan than Naomi is."

"A crime of passion," Kate answered.

Nathan nodded, but he still looked a little troubled. "There's something that doesn't fit with all this. The ritual and occult aspect of it."

"Yeah, that is a bump in the road. I'm not sure how to account for it either."

"There is one possibility..." Nathan suggested.

"Oh?"

"Joanna is clearly something of a socialite. She's well off, attractive, and is friends with some of the local movers and shakers," Nathan said, navigating to a folder on his computer filled with screenshots. He opened them up to show photos clearly taken at various events with people being handed awards or large cheques while dressed in their finery. In each photo, Joanna was there, smiling away at the heart of the action.

"What are you saying?"

"Look, I agree. I'm not sure she could, on her own, drag Jordan out to that tree and string him up. But if she had help. Help from people who might have some interest in ritual and secrecy..."

"You're suggesting a conspiracy?"

"We know they exist," he said, looking at her.

"Do we?" Kate asked, eyebrows raised.

"The Freemasons. Skull and Bones in the US. They're everywhere."

"And you think there's one in Surrey?" she asked, as she started to see some of what the other detectives had warned her about.

"I'm certain of it. I've been tracking their activities for months. Years even. We have unexplained disappearances, accidents, cover-ups. It happens all the time, but it's never investigated, and whenever someone gets close, they either disappear or suddenly lose interest."

"But not you. You won't be bought," Kate said.

"They demoted me," Nathan replied, his voice flat.

"They? You mean your superiors."

Nathan nodded, his eyes darting around the room.

Kate narrowed her eyes and felt like she was seeing Nathan in a new light. Witnessing a side of him that she hadn't seen before. Those in power certainly wanted to keep a hold of that power and would fight to keep it, but to accuse them of conspiracy felt like a step too far. "Alright, why don't we put that to one side for a moment. Let's forget this conspiracy thing for now and focus on who actually killed Jordan. We can worry about everything else later."

Nathan sat back. "You don't believe me."

Kate took a breath. "I'm not saying that. I'm saying we need to solve this case. We can talk about everything else another time."

Nathan looked at her for a long moment and then gave her a curt nod. "Alright. Fair enough."

"Good. I think we need to talk to both of these ladies," Kate said, ignoring the feeling of slight unease that sprouted up around her feelings towards Nathan.

"I'll get Naomi called in for this afternoon," Nathan said. "In the meantime, how about we pay Joanna a little visit?"

CHAPTER 17

"Let's tread carefully, shall we?" Kate said, turning to Nathan as he pulled the handbrake on.

With the car stopped just outside the Donaldson household, Nathan looked up at her, his expression innocent.

Kate gave him a look, raising her eyebrows at him.

"I will. I'll be sensitive," he said.

"And don't bring up any of this conspiracy talk either."

"What are you, my mum? Jeez. I'm not five years old, you know. I only told you that because, for some unknown bloody reason, I actually trust you. A bit."

Kate felt surprised, and her expression broadcast it clearly. "You trust me? Well, I am flattered."

"Don't get any ideas."

Kate smirked. "And here I was thinking I'd finally get into your pants."

"In your dreams, young lady," Nathan answered in mock indignation.

"Nightmares more like," Kate replied, her tone level.

"You're not wrong," Nathan replied as he climbed out of the car.

Kate followed suit and shut the door behind her. They were on the opposite side of the road from the house, and there were a couple of media vans parked up the street with a few reporters and photographers stood around outside the house.

"Parasites," Nathan stated.

"They're just doing their job, like us," Kate replied. She wasn't a fan of them either, but they had their uses.

"Come on, let's get through them and into the house."

Kate nodded as the first reporter approached them and began to ask questions.

"Have there been any developments in the case, detectives?"

"Are the reports on the occult nature of the killing accurate?" another asked.

"Any new leads?" said a third.

Kate ignored the questions, keeping pace with Nathan as they crossed the quiet street, making for the house.

"What's a disgraced officer like you doing on this case?" one of the reporters asked. Kate looked over to see Nathan's hackles rise and she recognised the reporter. It was Chester Longstaff, with his usual superior expression written large across his face.

"Does the victim's family know about your history?"

Kate grabbed Nathan's arm as he slowed, sensing his rising anger, and dragged him on. He followed, moving past Chester, towards the house.

A uniformed officer stood in the middle of the driveway and nodded as he checked their identification, letting them through.

The reporters continued to shout questions as they walked up the driveway, but they were finally away from them.

"You alright?" Kate asked.

"I'm fine," Nathan answered, his voice clipped.

Kate slowed him down. "Don't go in there all angry because of some idiot reporter. We need to do this right."

"You lead the conversation, Kate. You're better with people than I am."

"You're not that bad," she answered, trying to comfort him.

"Whatever. I need to cool down anyway," Nathan explained.

"Alright," Kate answered, acquiescing to Nathan's suggestion as she crossed the last few metres to the house. As they drew nearer, the door opened, revealing DC Faith Evanson stood just inside.

"They've been there all through the night since yesterday," she commented.

"Morning, Faith," Nathan said in greeting, and then lowered his voice to a whisper. "How is she today?"

Faith nodded. "Alright. She's in the kitchen at the back of the house."

Nathan nodded. Kate glanced back at the reporters, still making a nuisance of themselves at the end of the driveway. She felt like she'd probably keep away from the windows at the front of the house as well, if she were being harassed by the press.

"Hi, Kate. Are you well?" Faith asked.

"Surviving," she replied with a wry smile and followed Nathan through the house. They found Joanna sat at the kitchen table, nursing a hot drink and looking slightly stressed.

She greeted them dispassionately and invited them to sit. Kate sat beside Nathan on the opposite side of the table from Joanna, while Faith stood to one side, watching.

"How are you coping?" Kate asked as she settled into the chair.

Joanna shrugged. "As well as can be expected, I guess. Are you any closer to catching the bastard that did this?"

Kate cringed slightly at the language, sensing the other woman's pain and frustration. "We're following up on our leads, Mrs Donaldson. We can't say much more than that."

She nodded, looking disappointed.

"Along those lines," Kate continued, "we do have a few more questions for you."

"Sure, go ahead. I'll help if I can."

"Thank you, Mrs Donaldson, and I'm sorry if these are awkward questions, but I'm sure you understand, we need to follow up everything."

"Yes, yes. Go on, ask what you need to," Joanna said, sounding frustrated.

"Mrs Donaldson, we have good evidence that Jordan was having an affair in the last few months of this life," Kate said, watching Joanna's face closely.

Her eyes narrowed, and she regarded Kate and Nathan suspiciously, pressing her lips together as she tensed. "An affair?"

"That's correct."

"With who?"

"I think you know who," Kate answered, curious to see what she could draw out of her.

"And what on earth makes you think that?" she asked. The tone of her voice had risen, betraying how tense she was.

"We have emails from a personal account of Jordan's to another woman that are quite explicit."

"Just emails? That's your evidence?"

"Part of it. We also have an eyewitness who says they saw Jordan kissing the same woman."

"I see..." she answered, her eyes turning glassy and wet, before looking away from them.

"We also have CCTV showing your car outside the office on the night of Jordan's murder," Kate finished.

Joanna looked up as the first tears fell. "Oh..." she muttered, the defiance in her voice fading.

"Would you care to elaborate for us?" Nathan asked.

"Shit," Joanna cursed quietly, looking away. Kate raised an eyebrow and glanced at Nathan, wondering where this was going to lead. Was she the murderer?

They waited for her, but Joanna said nothing for the best part of a minute until Kate chose to finally press her.

"Joanna," she said, using her first name for the first time. "What did you know?"

Joanna closed her eyes and sighed, and the fight seemed to finally drain out of her. More tears fell as she looked up at Kate and Nathan. "I knew," she said.

"You knew what?"

"I knew he was having an affair... No, that's not right. I suspected."

"Why did you suspect it?" Nathan asked.

"Look. Things haven't been great between us since this," she said, patting her tummy. "The pregnancy was a mistake. We didn't mean for it to happen. Jordan was supposed to be focusing on his work, and we'd try for a baby later, but…"

"But what?"

She looked uncomfortable and shifted in her seat, as though there was something within her she wanted to let out and admit to, but wasn't sure if she should. She glanced up at them and then took another deep breath.

"I stopped taking the pill. I tricked him. I just wanted a baby. I couldn't wait. I thought it would be okay. I thought he'd be fine with it, you know? He'd be a great dad. I knew he wanted one eventually, so, I figured why not now? I didn't know it would lead to all this. I didn't mean to drive him away."

"He didn't like the fact that you got pregnant?" Kate asked.

"The pill isn't one hundred percent effective, so I said it must have been one of those things. You know?"

"Did you argue?"

Joanna nodded. "Yeah. He wanted me to get rid of it, but I wasn't going to do that. He didn't like that. I guess he felt betrayed," she explained. "He wasn't wrong."

"So, what happened?"

"That's when Naomi joined the business. She'd joined a month earlier in fact, but I didn't find out until after I fell pregnant. I don't go to the office much, but I couldn't believe it when I walked in to see her there."

"You knew her, then?"

"We were all at school together. Well, Naomi was at another school, a girl's school, but in the same year. Jordan dated her for a while before we got together, so I guess seeing her rekindled that old flame."

"So, you knew? About the affair, I mean?" Kate asked.

"Not at that point. I mean, I didn't like her being there, but I didn't know for sure that something was going on. Jordan often worked late. Had done for years, but I guess that's where they got together."

"So, why were you at the office that night?"

Joanna took another deep breath and let it out slowly. "Jordan was in the shower that morning, before going to work, and I saw a text come through from Naomi saying she'd see him later that night at work. So I asked him. I asked if he was working alone that night. He said he was."

"You caught him in a lie," Kate stated.

"Like you did with me," Joanna shrugged. "I was angry all day. Just furious. I wanted to catch them in the act. I sat outside the office, waiting, thinking of everything I'd say to them, and then Naomi pulled in, right in front of me. She didn't see me. But I couldn't do it. I couldn't face them. I was scared of losing him, and with the baby on the way, I didn't know what to do. So I left. Came home and cried myself to sleep."

"Is there any way to prove you were at home? Did you see anyone or speak to anyone?"

"I sent a message to a girlfriend saying I needed to talk, but that's all."

"That might be enough to triangulate your phone and prove your whereabouts. We'll look into it."

"Okay," she said, looking utterly defeated. All the fight had been taken out of her as the lies she'd told were laid bare. Tears continued to fall as she sat there, staring at the wall.

Her hand lashed out and smacked the coffee mug off the table onto the floor with a crash. "Bastard," she hissed through gritted teeth before breaking down and burying her head in her hands. Faith rushed forwards to comfort her.

Now that the truth was out, Kate sat back and shared a look with Nathan.

"I'm sorry," Joanna said through her sobs. "I know I lied. To you, I mean. But I was worried about how it would look if I told you that I knew about the affair. I'd look guilty. I'm the wronged party, the one who had the biggest motive to kill him. But I couldn't do that. I'd never…"

"Do you know why someone might want to kill him?" Kate asked.

Joanna shook her head. "Sorry, no. No idea. He was a lovely man. I don't know anyone who held a grudge against him."

"Okay, Mrs Donaldson," Kate said and looked over at Nathan again with a questioning look.

"Mrs Donaldson, we'll leave this for now. You've answered our questions to our satisfaction. We'll keep you informed of the progress of our investigation, of course," Nathan said as he pushed his chair back and stood up.

"Thank you," Joanna said. "For everything. I really appreciate it."

"We may need to speak to you again soon, at the station," Kate warned her.

"I understand."

CHAPTER 18

"So, if Naomi and Jordan were having an affair, and Joanna knew about it, but did nothing, who did? Who killed Jordan?"

"I think we need to talk to Naomi again and find out what she knows. She might well talk once she realises the game is up."

"Once she realises we know she lied, you mean. Yeah, maybe..." Kate mused as she gazed out the window at the passing countryside. "It's more likely to be a boyfriend or former partner of hers though, isn't it, really?"

"I would say so."

"So, this Steve then, maybe. Her ex."

Nathan nodded. "Unless there's anyone else that she's not telling us about."

"The endless lies are a little grating. I wish people would just tell the truth."

"It would certainly make our investigations much easier."

They soon made it back to the station in the village and to the Murder Team's office. As they approached their two desks, Kate noticed the SOCO, Sheridan sat in Nathan's chair, waiting for them. She smiled as they approached and waved a file in the air at them.

"Got something for you," Sheridan said.

"Oooh, excellent. What is it?" Nathan asked.

"Just the report from the sweep of the office in Guildford. There are a few interesting findings you might be interested in."

"Excellent," Nathan answered her, waving her out of his chair.

Sheridan stood up, allowing Nathan to sit and handed him the report. "Looks like your investigation is going well," she said, pointing to the big board with its various photos and post-it notes stuck to it, linked by black marker lines and scribbled words.

"We're making progress," Kate said.

"Good, and how are you finding working with this old coot?" Sheridan asked her while Nathan opened the report and began to scan it.

"Good. It's been a full-on first few days, that's for sure, but I think we work well together."

"Mmmm, do you indeed? Did you hear that, Nathan? She likes working with you."

He looked up at the Scene Of Crime Officer. "They all do. They just won't admit it, of course."

"Nice to see you've maintained your humble perspective," Sheridan replied.

"Quiet, peasant, I'm reading."

Sheridan rolled her eyes. Last time Kate had seen her, she'd been wearing one of the white forensic jumpsuits, which were not very flattering, and only showed her eyes, which had been behind protective glasses as well.

Today, she wore the dark outfit of a Forensic Officer, and for the first time Kate saw her whole face and her blonde hair, tied back in a ponytail.

"Please, go ahead and summarise for us anyway," Kate said to Sheridan. "I'm listening, even if he isn't."

"Alright. The only real significant finds were in his office. We found traces of blood, which we matched with Jordan's blood, and also traces of Jordan's semen. There were also some dark fibres there which we matched to fibres we found at the murder site, linking the two locations. We couldn't find any matching boot prints to the ones we found at the murder site though."

"And, DNA?"

"Matches for all the staff were found, as well as several others who we know had visited the office, or were in the office when we arrived. We didn't find any traces of Mr Norman's DNA though."

"Well, that helps to rule out Robyn's boyfriend," Kate said to Nathan.

"It does. Thank you, Sheridan, excellent work, as always."

"Pleasure. I'll catch you later. Hope to see you again soon," she said to Kate, who smiled and nodded back.

She sat back in her chair and considered the additional evidence. "So, now we know for sure that the killer kidnapped Jordan from the office," Kate said.

Nathan turned to look at her, leaving the forensic file on his desk. "We also have Naomi's car behind the office for twenty minutes that night. That doesn't mean it's her though. There's another entrance to that rear loading area further along the street which we don't have coverage of, but it's very suspicious that she was there, out of sight for twenty minutes."

"Looks like there's evidence of a struggle if there are traces of Jordan's blood."

"And sexual activity," Nathan added.

"They probably used that office for their late-night encounters," Kate agreed. "If Naomi was able to gain access to the office that night, she would have no trouble distracting him."

"So, do you think she did it?" Nathan asked.

"If she did, I doubt she did it on her own. Maybe with this ex of hers? Steve? Any luck in finding him?"

"Nothing so far. We have no idea where he is."

"Gaffer wants an update," DI Sam Mason said, wandering over. "Anything from your visit to Joanna? Is she an alien, perhaps?" he suggested with a sneer aimed at Nathan.

"She admitted to knowing about an affair between Naomi and her husband," Kate said.

"Motive," Mason answered.

"And she was at the office on the night of the murder, but only briefly."

"Opportunity," Mason said.

"I'm not sure I'd agree with that," Kate challenged him. "She was there, but didn't stay and didn't leave her car, which is clearly visible in the footage we have. Otherwise, she was at home, and she says she was texting her friends, so we should have a record of that to give us an idea of where she was, based on the signal masts she was using."

"So, if it's not her, then?"

"We've invited Naomi in for a talk," Nathan said.

"I am aware. And speaking of which, she's here and waiting downstairs," Sam informed them.

"So, maybe you could have led with that?" Nathan suggested.

"Maybe, but where would the fun be in that?"

"Thank you, DI Mason," Kate said.

Sam smiled at her. "Let me know how it goes," he said and wandered off in the direction of his desk.

"Such a dick," Nathan muttered to her once Sam was out of earshot.

"I can't say I disagree, but I'm not about to rub him the wrong way this early in my new job. Come on, let's go speak with Miss Sawyer."

CHAPTER 19

Walking into the interview room, Kate looked over at the slim form of Naomi, sitting on the opposite side of the table, and saw a more nervous and vulnerable version of the woman than she'd seen before.

When she'd come in for her first interview, she'd been focused and keen to help, but this time, she did not look quite so sure.

Kate thought calling these things interviews was something of a misnomer though. The word 'interview' suggested that the two sides were coming to the meeting as equals, about to discuss an exchange of ideas. But this was almost never the case.

A better term, Kate thought, would be an interrogation. It was a more accurate term, and better described the dynamic that took place during these meetings.

The interviewer—the police—wanted to know something, and the interviewee potentially had that info. So it was down to them to draw it out of people like Naomi.

And that was probably why Naomi looked so nervous.

She'd already been here. She'd already answered their questions, and yet, here she was again. It wouldn't take a genius to guess that they wanted something more.

If she'd lied, as they believed she had, then it was likely Naomi was nervous about revealing something she wanted to keep quiet.

At least, that's what Kate hoped. She hoped that Naomi had something useful or interesting to tell them. Something that might propel their case forward and lead to some kind of breakthrough.

"Miss Sawyer, thank you for coming in today. We just have a few more questions for you regarding the death of Jordan Donaldson based on information that we have since acquired," Nathan said. "I will be interviewing you under caution, though, meaning you do not have to say anything. But it may harm your defence if you do not mention when questioned, something which you later rely on in court. Anything you do say may be given in evidence."

"Am I in trouble?" she asked.

Kate got the feeling she'd had chats with the police before, chats that might have not been very friendly.

"No," Kate answered quickly, making sure to get that in before Nathan said anything. Right now, Naomi wasn't in trouble, so it wasn't a lie, but if something came up during this interrogation, then that could, of course, change.

"So, I could leave if I wanted?"

"Should you wish to," Kate answered, and stole a quick glance at Nathan, who was watching Naomi intensely. "You're not under arrest, and we can provide you with a solicitor if you like."

Naomi looked between them and then nodded. "No, I'm fine. Alright. How can I help?"

Kate took her seat beside Nathan, opposite Naomi, and readied her notebook. She also opened up a laptop she'd taken from the office upstairs, and logged in, preparing a key piece of evidence.

Looking up at Nathan, he nodded for her to begin.

"How are you holding up?" Kate asked, choosing a soft approach to begin with, given Naomi's clear nervousness.

Naomi nodded. "I'm okay," she replied with a brief smile

"I know it's difficult. Losing someone is never easy," Kate sympathised.

Naomi gave her a smile and nodded. "I just don't understand why someone would do this to him. Jordan's been nothing but good to people. I don't know anyone who'd have anything against him."

"Oh?" Kate answered. "What about your ex, Steve?"

Naomi seemed to come up short as she opened her mouth to answer, but no reply was forthcoming.

"Seems to me that he might have a problem with Jordan."

Naomi frowned. "And why's that?" she asked, as she seemed to overcome her surprise and regain her composure. "Why would having a job cause Steve to get jealous?"

"Naomi. You were more than just an employee for Jordan, weren't you?"

"I'm quite sure I don't know what you mean," Naomi protested, looking somewhat scandalised.

"You didn't go to the office the other night just to work, did you?" Nathan asked, joining in the questioning.

"You were there for something more… intimate," Kate pressed.

Naomi pulled a shocked expression. "How dare you!"

"We know you were having an affair with Jordan, Naomi. We've seen the emails between you two, we have an eyewitness who saw you kissing, and then there's the DNA evidence."

Naomi frowned, staring at Kate as she spoke.

"It's easier if you admit to it, Naomi. We know what you two were doing, and if you lie to us now, it's just going to make us more suspicious of you. After all, why lie, unless you have something to hide?" Kate asked.

"I don't have anything to hide. I'm not the killer."

"Good, I hope not. But if you have nothing to hide, then you won't mind being a little more forthcoming about your relationship with Jordan, and what was really going on between you two."

Naomi let out a dramatic sigh, as if this was the biggest inconvenience of her life, and looked to the ceiling.

"Alright, fine. Yes, Jordan and I were seeing either other. Alright? Is that what you want to hear?"

"That's part of it," Nathan answered.

"How long had it been going on?" Kate continued.

"A few months. We'd flirted for a while after I took the job. It was nice, you know? Brought back memories of what it had been like at school. Back before we had all these responsibilities. I don't think either of us meant for it to go any further."

"But it did," Kate stated.

"Yeah. I was just in his office one day, going over something to do with work. I can't remember what. A lettings agreement or something. Anyway, we got close, our hands touched, and one thing led to another..." Naomi explained, smiling at the memory.

"But it didn't stop there?"

"We pulled apart fairly quickly. I guess Jordan felt guilty. I did too. I knew he was married. But it happened again not long after."

"Didn't you feel bad, knowing he had a wife?"

She sighed again. "Yeah. I did. Probably not as bad as he did, but yeah, I didn't feel good about it. I couldn't stop myself, though. It was fun. Dangerous. I enjoyed it."

"Then you worked late with him one night?"

She nodded. "It was only about two weeks after that first kiss. It became our thing. We'd meet up at the office, do a little work if it needed doing, and then spend some time together in his office."

"And you didn't try to call it off?"

"Yeah, he did. But I guess he couldn't stop himself."

"And you didn't want to stop?"

Naomi shrugged with a thin smile. "I liked him. I liked the intimacy. He was gentle and kind, and just not at all like Steve."

"And yet, you lied to us about it. Why?" Nathan asked.

Naomi seemed to deflate as her train of thought switched tracks. "Because of Steve. He never did really stop harassing me, but it did die down. I saw him around a bit. Here and there. He'd follow me..." She paused as if she had difficulty talking about it.

"What happened between you two?" Kate asked. "You said you met Steve at school?" Kate hoped that by getting her to think about her early days with Steve, and tell the story, all the details would spill out of her.

Naomi nodded. "We were great together at first. Steve was a beautiful young man when we first met. Full of ambition and drive to make a name for himself. He wanted to be a chef, you know. He was so good at cooking.

"Did Jordan and Steve know each other?" Kate asked, hoping she wasn't pushing her luck by asking the question.

"Yeah. They did. We all kind of knew each other. I mean, I went to a different school, but we met up before and after, and in later years when we were allowed out at lunch break we'd see each other then. So, yeah, they knew each other."

"Were they friends?" Kate asked.

"I don't know about that. I think Steve was a bit scared of Jordan, actually. Jordan was taller and into sports. Steve liked cooking. I think Jordan might have thought of Steve as a bit of a wimp."

"Did Jordan bully him?"

"Um, no. I don't think so. There was banter and jokes. You know, that kind of thing. We all did it, though. It was just harmless fun, no one wanted to hurt anyone."

"You all did it?" Nathan asked.

"Yeah. We made fun of each other. It was just kids being kids, though."

"So, school came to an end, and then what?" Kate continued.

"After school, Steve pursued his dream and became a chef. Later he bought his own restaurant and ran his own business. But it didn't work out as he hoped it would. The business began to fail, and he turned to drink. That's when he started to get violent. I didn't stay long after that. We separated."

"But he didn't leave you alone?" Kate asked.

"No, he didn't."

"That's when you logged those complaints with us?"

"That's right," Naomi replied. "He'd follow me, confront me, get abusive. I just wanted to get away from him."

"Where did you go?" Kate asked.

"To a women's shelter," she answered, looking into the middle distance as she thought back. "Those were better times. He couldn't get to me there. I was safe. He backed off eventually, but I couldn't stay. The shelter had some arrangements with property developers so those of us that were able, could try to move on. So, that's what I did. I got the job at Donaldson's shortly after that."

"And Steve?" Nathan inquired.

"He found me. I don't know how. Maybe he saw me in town or something, but he confronted me a little while ago and has been making a nuisance of himself ever since."

"Is he violent?" Kate asked.

"He hasn't been since the shelter."

"Does he know where you live?"

"I don't think so. He knows where I work, though."

"I see," Kate replied, suspicion in her voice. "So, he must have recognised Jordan?"

"Yeah, maybe, I guess," Naomi replied.

"Do you know where Steve lives these days?"

"Not really, no. But he looks a mess. Like, really a mess. He stinks too. I keep thinking that maybe he's homeless."

"Or living in a squat or shelter?" Nathan suggested.

Naomi nodded. "Yeah, maybe."

"What about the occult?" Kate asked.

"The what?" Naomi looked confused at her question, frowning at her.

"Does Steve have any interest in the occult?"

"What do you mean by occult?" Naomi didn't seem any the wiser.

"I mean like witchcraft, Paganism, ghosts?"

"What's that got to do with this?" Naomi replied.

"The killer appears to have killed Jordan in a manner that suggests some occult knowledge. Has Steve ever expressed an interest in the occult?" Nathan asked.

"Um, not that I'm aware of... No, wait. We did do some of that séance stuff back in school. You know, just silly stuff, like moving a cup around a board as we asked questions. It's all codswallop though, isn't it," Naomi said.

"So, he knew a little about the occult?" Nathan continued.

"I don't know. I never saw anything like that while we were married. He didn't seem interested in that kind of thing at all."

"Could he have kept that interest hidden from you?"

Naomi shrugged. "I guess if he had really wanted to."

"What about the affair between you and Jordan. Could he have known about that?"

"I don't know. Maybe? I know he was watching the office. I noticed him hanging around outside a couple of times. He might have read into things."

"Alright," Nathan answered.

"You think he killed Jordan, don't you?" Naomi accused them.

"Someone did, and right now, the one with the biggest motive is Steve."

"I can see how you'd think that," Naomi replied.

Kate frowned. "And you don't?"

"Alright, yes, he was a little violent with me a couple of times, but I honestly don't think he'd kill someone. That's just not him, you know?"

"Can you be sure?" Kate asked.

"How can you be sure about anything in life? No, I can't be sure. Maybe he's gone full psycho, but that was not the man I knew."

"When you first met him, did you think he was capable of hitting you?" Nathan asked, pressing the issue.

"Alright, no, I guess not," Naomi conceded.

"So how can you be sure he wouldn't kill someone if he were pushed far enough?"

Naomi shrugged. "No, you're right. I guess we've all got it in us."

Nathan nodded. "Jealousy can make people do some pretty crazy things."

CHAPTER 20

"Does he look the part to you?" Kate asked as they made their way back up to the team's main room. She held up her phone which had a photo of Steve Brewster on it that Naomi had texted to her.

"What do killers look like, really? They can be anyone," Nathan said.

"Alright, smart arse. Do you think he did it? Do you think he killed Jordan?"

"It's all looking pretty damning, isn't it?" Nathan answered as they climbed the stairs.

Kate stopped showing the photo to Nathan and took one final look at the image. "We need to find him and quickly."

"We've got officers out there looking for him," Nathan said.

"I think we need to do more than that, though. He could be anywhere. It could be days before we find him. He might kill again before then."

"So, what do you suggest?"

"There's media interest in this murder, so let's use that. Let's get the press to work for us."

"You want to issue a statement to them and give them Steve's picture?"

"Do you have a better idea?"

Nathan grumbled as they approached the door to their office space. "We're checking out all the local squats and places that the homeless tend to gather. We've got plenty of people on the job."

"You know as well as I do, that we probably don't know half the squats in this city, nor all the places where the homeless sleep," Kate countered.

Nathan grumbled, muttering something, but Kate couldn't make out what he was saying.

"You know I'm right on this. Look, I know you don't like the press, but they do have their uses."

"Alright, fine. Let's do it. We'll issue a statement to the press and give them the photo."

"Who's issuing a statement to the press?" Kate looked up to see DI Mason walking over. They'd been crossing the Murder Team's main office, making for their desks as they talked.

"We need to find someone. Naomi's ex-husband, Steven Brewster. We have reason to suspect that he might be the killer, but we have no idea where he might be."

"None at all?"

"We think he's homeless, so maybe he's in a squat somewhere."

"We have officers on that right now though, don't we?" Sam asked.

"We do, sir," Kate replied. "But I think this might go a lot smoother and quicker if we use the press to our advantage. Someone out there will know where Steve is."

"I have expressed my reservations about this to DC O'Connell," Nathan said.

Sam looked over at Nathan. "Have you?" He seemed to consider this for a moment, and then looked back at Kate. "Well, I think you might be right, Kate. I think leveraging the press is a great idea."

Kate smiled at her superior officer and glanced sideways at Nathan who'd stepped back, out of Sam's eyeline. He winked at her.

Had he just manipulated Sam into agreeing with her plan?

"Thank you, sir," Kate replied, looking back at DI Mason.

"As it's your idea, how about you read the statement to the press?"

Kate's smile dropped from her face. "Um, me sir?"

"Why not? It's your idea. I'm sure you can draft a statement and read it out to them."

Kate's mind raced at the thought of going out there and talking to the media. She'd never done such a thing before, but she guessed now was as good a time as any. It was her idea, after all. Still, as much as she tried to rationalise it in her own mind, her body had ideas of its own as her heart rate increased and the butterflies took flight in her belly.

"I guess so," Kate answered, looking to Nathan for help.

Nathan gave her a thin smile and shrugged, spreading his hands wide, palms upturned. He could have stepped in and insisted that he do it instead of her, given he'd been on the force much longer than she had, but he'd already made his own dislike for the press quite clear, and she guessed he would not be stepping up to take this off her hands.

"Good. I think you'll do a great job representing this department, Kate. I'll look forward to watching it. I'll get everything arranged for you and let you know what time you're speaking to them. All you need to do is prepare your statement. Alright?"

"Should I take questions?" Kate asked, feeling unsure how these things were usually handled. She'd seen enough of them on TV though, so maybe this wouldn't be the shit-show she feared.

"I'll leave that up to you," DI Mason replied with a flicker of a smile. "Go prepare your statement, I'll be in touch shortly."

Kate nodded and moved towards her desk and Nathan. "He did that on purpose, didn't he?"

Nathan nodded. "I think so, yes. Maybe he doesn't like you working with me, or it's his way of getting to me."

"Does he think he might get you to take over for me?"

"That could be what he's hoping for."

"You're not going to do that though, are you?" Kate asked.

"Sorry, no. I hate these things. Besides, I'm confident you'll do a great job of it."

Kate smiled back at him. "Thanks, I guess."

"Don't be nervous. You'll do just fine," Nathan said to her with a smile. "You'd better get writing that statement though. If I know Sam, he'll arrange the conference to start in like, ten minutes or something ridiculous, just to try to get me to step in."

"Right," Kate said, sitting down at her computer. A strange determination washed over her as she opened a blank document, and she realised she actually didn't want Nathan to do it for her. She wanted to do this herself. She felt like she wanted to prove to herself, and to everyone else, that she had the balls to do what was needed.

True to form, Sam arranged the press conference to start as early as he could. Luckily, the setting up of the podium and the microphones seemed to stop him from giving her just ten minutes to prepare.

As it turned out, she had forty minutes to draft her statement, which was more than enough time to get everything ready. She even managed to read the thing through a few times to get it lodged in her brain somewhere.

Getting up, Kate brushed off her jacket with her hand and pulled it back on over her shirt.

"I'll come with you," Nathan said, standing up from his desk.

"You don't have to," she said, adjusting her clothing and hair.

"I know. But look, if you really want me to do this for you, I will. I don't mind."

"Thanks, but no, I've said I'll do this. I want to see it through," Kate replied, making sure she sounded firm and not nervous, despite how she felt inside.

"Okay, but I'll be right next to you. Just give me a nudge if you want some help."

Kate nodded. "Thanks."

"No problem," Nathan replied, crossing the room with her. As she walked, she spotted DCI Dean approaching her. He waved her down.

"Skipper," Kate said in greeting as she stopped just before him.

"DI Mason was a little overzealous putting you up to this," he said. "We'll get this changed as I don't think tha…"

"I'm fine, sir," Kate cut in. "Sorry to interrupt, but I want to do this. I'm aware of the potential reasons why DI Mason put me up to this, but honestly, I can do this."

"Are you sure?"

"Positive."

The DCI relaxed onto his heels and gave her an appraising look. "Alright, if you're sure."

"I am," Kate replied.

"She'll do just fine," Nathan added, backing her up. The DCI let her go, and the pair walked down towards the front of the building where the press was waiting for her.

"You've got your statement ready?" Nathan asked, fussing over her like a protective mother.

"Yeah, I'm ready for them," she answered him, finding his concern cute.

"Don't let your guard down. This is the press we're talking about here. They'll eat you alive if you give an inch," he said.

"Speaking from experience?" she asked, genuinely curious.

"I just know what they can be like," he answered her. "Just stick to the script, don't be tempted to ad-lib, and you'll be fine."

"What about taking questions?" She wasn't sure on the etiquette of this.

"I'd urge you not to go down that road. That's when things can get nasty. Ultimately, it's up to you though, but I think you'd be better off avoiding that altogether."

Kate nodded, understanding his concern, but she was also well aware of his feelings towards the media and wondered if that was tainting his answer to her question. She guessed she could call an end to the press conference whenever she wanted though, so if things got uncomfortable, she'd just walk out.

They reached the main front entrance and could see the crowd of reporters outside, stood before a small podium that was sprouting microphones from every inch of it.

The butterflies in her stomach really began to flutter as she paused to take a breath, and build up the last bit of courage she could muster.

A man walked over, one of the civilian workers in the building who looked to be waiting for them. "Detective O'Connell?" he inquired.

Kate smiled. "That's me."

"Everything's ready for you out there. The mics are all live, so careful what you say."

"Okay, thanks," she said, and approached the entrance, where a couple of officers waited for her, and accompanied her out of the building. They stopped just outside the doors, guarding the entrance and flanking her, ready in case it got a little rough.

She approached the podium with Nathan behind her, hanging back as the media people pressed in towards her. Several of them were already asking questions, but she simply ignored them and placed her prepared statement on the podium.

"Thank you for coming today. I'm Detective O'Connell, one of the officers working on the Donaldson murder case. We've made significant progress, and inquiries are ongoing, so you'll understand that we are unable to discuss the details of the case at this time. However, we do have someone we need to find and speak to, which is the reason for coming out here to speak with you today," she said.

Her heart was hammering away inside her chest as she spoke, but she concentrated on the words and kept her pace measured, trying not to talk too quickly. As the sentences passed, her nerves began to ease, and she started to settle into the moment.

"The man we're looking for is Steve Brewster," she continued, holding up a printed photo of Steve.

"He's a local man who we believe to be living rough or squatting somewhere. We're keen to speak with him and to eliminate him from the investigation, but have been unable to locate him so far. If you know where he is, I would urge you not to approach him, and to get in touch with the Surrey Police Service, or Crime Stoppers as soon as you can."

She looked up from her statement, and a second later, questions filled the air from the gathered reporters. The sheer number and force with which the press threw the questions at her took her by surprise, and she almost stumbled backwards. But she recovered quickly, and after a moment, decided that she would attempt to answer some of them.

Amidst the chaos, she heard someone close to her ask a question she could answer.

"When will the Donaldson's Estate Agents reopen?"

"That's a question for them," Kate replied, bringing the reporters to silence again as she spoke. It was like she held some kind of power over them, and she quite liked the feel of it.

"What of the reports that the death was some kind of satanic sacrifice?" someone called out the second she'd finished answering the previous question.

"I can't answer that, inquiries are ongoing," she answered, hoping that her stoic reply would stop them asking probing questions like that.

"Is this related to the disappearance of Mark Summers?" someone else asked. Kate turned to see Chester Longstaff stood nearby, staring at her after asking this latest question. The gathered press went quiet to hear her answer.

"There's nothing to suggest the two are linked," she answered, and was then unsure if she'd said the right thing.

"How long have you been a serving, Detective?" someone else called out.

"What can you tell us about Jordan's affair with Naomi Sawyer?" someone else added.

Kate took half a step back, surprised that these details had leaked to the press already, and unsure how to answer. Nathan stepped up beside her. "Thank you, no more questions," Nathan said into the mics, and took Kate by the arm, guiding her away from the podium.

She didn't resist, and with a smile to the assembled press, turned to walk back inside.

"What's it like working with a disgraced detective?" It was the distinctive voice of Chester Longstaff. Kate looked back and caught Chester's knowing smile as he waited for her answer, but he'd never get it. She walked back into the building and let out a long sigh.

"Well, that felt like a car crash and a half," Kate commented.

"Rubbish. You did well," Nathan reassured her. "You handled yourself professionally, and I think you represented the force well out there."

"But I froze at the end."

"It probably felt worse than it really was. Trust me, you did well. I think the skipper will be happy with that."

"Okay, if you say so," she answered, not quite believing him, but appreciating his support for what she felt was an amateurish performance. They headed back upstairs and to the main room where there was a small crowd gathered around one of the TVs. As she walked back into the office, a cheer went up from the team, peppered with applause.

Kate blushed and paused as she smiled at the other officers.

She noticed Nathan give her a smile and walk off as several others approached her, including DCI Dean.

"Well done, congratulations. You did well out there," he said as Claire, Rachel, and a couple other officers stepped up to her.

"That was amazing," Rachel added.

"I think that deserves a celebratory cake tomorrow," Claire added, to Kate's amusement. Was everything about baking and cakes with her?

"You looked good out there, O'Connell," Sam Mason added, walking over. "We should put you in front of the camera more often."

Kate wasn't sure if she should be offended by the comment or not, as it sounded a little sexist, but she erred on the side of caution and merely smiled at DI Mason.

"Thanks," she said to everyone, feeling embarrassed by the attention.

"So, which conspiracy is this case all about then, hey?" another female detective asked.

Kate looked over, recognising DC Octavia Ash, another of the younger detectives on the team, and another with something of a grudge against Nathan.

Kate ignored the comment.

"Seriously, good work. Well done. Now, back to work, all of you," the DCI said, taking charge of the situation. Kate eyed Octavia who walked back towards her desk beside Sam, the pair of them joking to each other as they went.

"While you're partnering with me, you'll never be totally accepted by them," Nathan said as she approached her desk.

"Is that right?" she commented, returning to her seat, feeling somewhat defiant. She'd seen Nathan's interest in conspiracy, and she had to admit it was a little creepy, but there was something about his conviction in it. There was also something about the nature of this murder investigation that gave her pause and made her wonder just how real some of these theories of Nathan's were. Might some of them have links to the truth or a version of it?

Cults were real, after all. There were endless examples of groups of people doing some incredibly horrific things, including killing themselves in the name of some god or other. Not to mention killing other people.

All it took was one charismatic leader to whip his followers into a frenzy and make them believe what he was saying. So, just how wrong was Nathan about some of these ideas?

More importantly, how did they relate to this case?

The rest of the afternoon was taken up with paperwork until Kate could finally head home.

She walked into her small apartment in north Leatherhead and collapsed onto her sofa, feeling utterly shattered and drained from the day's events, not least of which being the press conference.

She shook her head as she thought back through those few minutes, and couldn't quite believe she'd done it. If someone had told her she'd be holding a press conference before the end of the week, she'd have told them they were crazy, and yet, here she was.

With a sigh she reached out, picked up the remote for the TV, and turned on the news. Right away, her face filled the screen as the local evening news reported on her press conference.

She eyed her appearance with a critical eye, deciding she looked tired and in need of a good night's rest, while also wondering if she really sounded like that.

With a grunt, she heaved herself out of the depths of her sofa and to the kitchen.

She needed something to eat.

CHAPTER 21

He stood a short distance away from the bank of monitors watching the screen, admiring the young detective. She'd had a busy day today, he thought as he watched her every move.

The press conference seemed to have gone well for her. She seemed tired but confident as she'd asked for help in finding the killer.

The man smiled to himself. Find him? Heh. They'd never find him in time. Not before he'd completed his masterwork anyway. He'd been too careful. Covered his tracks too well, giving them almost nothing to go on.

He was too good for them, and with the backing of his superiors, there really was little they could do. He felt sure of that.

He stood there and stared at the monitor a little longer, enjoying watching the young detective, and wondering if he might need to deal with her as well sometime.

He'd enjoy adding her to the list of people who'd made the ultimate sacrifice for him, helping him achieve his goals and the goals of the organisation.

But he had much more to do tonight and reluctantly turned away from the monitors to head for another room, pulling on his balaclava as he went.

In the middle of the next room, in the centre of the dirty floor, tied to the blood-stained bed, lay his ultimate and final victim. He'd spent weeks preparing him for this last moment, this final epiphany that he felt sure would propel him up to where he wanted to be.

The naked man lay on the sheets, covered in blood. Some of it was still fresh from the day's earlier activities, while other bits were weeks old, and were crumbling off his raw skin.

His captive looked up at him with wild, fear-filled eyes and flinched away as he drew near.

"Mark. Don't be afraid. The time is almost upon us," he said as he pulled out his ceremonial knife with its silver handle, encrusted with gleaming rubies.

"I have other work tonight, but before I do that, we need to get you ready for the final stage of this process."

Mark didn't answer him, he just looked up at his concealed face in mute horror, perhaps unable to say anything.

"You know what, I think we've come to know one another quite well over these past few weeks, you and I. So here, let's have no more secrets from each other," he said, and pulled off his balaclava, revealing the face beneath.

Mark looked shocked for a moment, and then, as the initial surprise drained away, his expression changed. Some kind of dawning realisation or recognition washed over Mark as he looked up.

"I... I know you..." Mark said, and the man smiled.

"Yes, you do," the man answered, and raised the knife into view. "Shall we get to know one another a little better?"

CHAPTER 22

Kate sat straight up in bed as her phone rang loudly from less than a metre away.

"Wha?" she gasped as she tried to figure out what on earth was going on. Was it her alarm? she wondered, reaching for her phone. She stared at the screen in confusion for a second before realising someone was calling her.

No, not someone. Nathan. Nathan was calling her.

She tapped answer and put the phone to her ear. "Hello?"

"Good, you're up," he said.

"No thanks to you," she grumbled. "What time is it?"

"Nearly five in the morning."

"So, four something or other... ugh. What is it?"

"There's been another murder."

Kate blinked. "What?" she asked, the shock of the statement banishing her grogginess in a second.

"Get up, I'm heading to yours. I'll be there in fifteen minutes. I'll fill you in on the way." Nathan ended the call, and for a second, Kate could only stare at her phone, wondering what was going on. She looked over at her clock to check the time and groaned at the number that glowed brightly on the screen.

"Aaaah, crap," she muttered swinging her legs over the side of the bed. Fifteen minutes, she thought. That wasn't long, but she felt confident she could shower, dress, and be ready in that time.

In the end, she was downstairs, pulling her still-wet hair up into a ponytail and waiting for Nathan with less than a minute to spare. She wished she'd had time to grab some breakfast, but figured she'd find something later.

Maybe Claire would bring some treats again today that she could indulge in.

At fifteen minutes and thirty-eight seconds, Nathan pulled up outside her building and she walked out to meet him. The air was still cool, but the sky was already beginning to lighten as dawn approached.

"Morning," Kate said, climbing into the passenger seat. "This is an ungodly hour to be going to work."

"Yeah, sorry about that. I'll put out a press release asking all criminals to only commit a crime during business hours. How's that?"

"That would be a start," she replied. "So, where are we heading?"

"Guildford. From what I've heard, Naomi Sawyer has been found dead."

"Naomi? Shit. Do you think it's our guy? The one who killed Jordan?"

"Don't know. I've not gotten any details through. I guess we'll find out more when we get there."

Kate nodded, thinking about their meeting with Naomi yesterday. She'd been a little nervous about the interview, but she'd still been full of life. She wondered what this would mean for their case if it was the same killer.

If nothing else, it was undoubtedly suspicious timing. That alone made it very likely that Naomi and Jordan's killers were one and the same.

She frowned, wondering what the pattern was, but she had too little to go on for the time being. They needed to get to the scene of the crime and have a look.

Traffic was light and they had no problem driving into town and making their way to Naomi's apartment, which was in a purpose-built development of flats on a residential road. The street was closed off with police cars everywhere, their blue lights flashing. Some of the local residents stood nearby, watching the events, and no doubt wondering what was going on.

They were shown through the police cordon before Nathan parked up. Kate climbed out and joined him as they made their way towards the building.

"Looks like the Cleaner's on duty again," Nathan commented, nodding ahead of them.

Kate followed his gaze to see Sergeant Louis Dyson approaching them and suddenly understood the nickname.

"This makes it two for two for you, I think," the sergeant commented.

"You think this is the same killer who murdered Jordan?" Kate asked him.

"You tell me, you're the brains department. But I can tell you it's another messy one. Grab a forensic suit from over there," he said, directing them to a nearby van. "I'll fill you in on the details once you're ready."

"If this is Naomi, then it's doubtful that she was involved in murdering Jordan," Kate said, pulling the protective suit over her clothes.

"It also casts greater suspicion on Joanna Donaldson, and on Naomi's former husband," Nathan suggested.

"I think you'll find the husband angle to be much more compelling," the sergeant said from where he stood a few metres away.

"Oh?" Nathan asked.

"We've taken a statement from a neighbour of Naomi's that saw her outside the building late last night. She was in an argument with her former husband, Steve Brewster. A pretty fiery one, according to the witness."

"And where's this witness?" Nathan asked.

"In a van, over there. We have a few officers with her. She was the one to find the body, too."

"We'll need to speak to her," Kate said.

The sergeant nodded. "Of course."

They finished getting prepared, pulling on gloves and the protective coverings over their shoes, before Sergeant Dyson showed them to an upstairs flat. Officers were everywhere, dusting down surfaces to lift prints using various techniques.

"The Divisional Surgeon has already attended and pronounced life extinct, and the photographer has made his pass as well. The pathologist has just finished up, and SOCO's are in there now," the sergeant explained to them as they walked.

The sergeant led them through the apartment into the small bedroom and the horror scene inside.

Naomi lay naked on the bed, her arms and legs spread wide, covered in cuts that looked very deliberate. Blood was everywhere, pooled on the bed, splattered over the floor, and up onto the walls, where some of it had been used to draw strange symbols, presumably with a finger.

In amongst the symbols and splatters was a single word that held particular meaning for Kate and Nathan.

'Today.'

The smell was bad in here and would only get worse as the decomposition continued. Kate took a deep breath as she took in the scene and the suffering that this young woman had been through.

She felt sorry for her, and as she surveyed the scene and the ritualistic nature of the killing, those same memories of her aunt's death bubbled up once more. She remembered the reports and the news stories she'd read that had documented her murder as a feeling of dizziness washed over her.

No sooner had the memories of her aunt surfaced, the memories of her actions quickly followed. Flashes of her confrontation with Duane in that Cork car park rose up like dark, angry spirits forcing her to steady herself against the nearby door frame. She squeezed her eyes shut and pushed the memories away and back. She hated herself for allowing them to take hold of her again, making her look weak and squeamish.

As the seconds passed, the feeling faded, and she soon got a hold of herself again and returned her attention to the room.

"Those look similar to the cuts on Jordan's body," Nathan commented, stepping closer to the body, apparently ignoring her moment of weakness.

Kate followed, inspecting the cuts. They weren't frenzied stab wounds, these were precise cuts as if the killer had been writing on her, using a knife like a pen, and her body as the canvas. They were also practically identical to the wounds on Jordan's body.

As with Jordan, a single stab wound to her heart looked like the killing blow.

"It's all very similar," said a familiar voice from their right. Kate looked up and recognised SOCO Sheridan Lane who'd just finished bagging a sample of blood. "With just a few key differences."

"Hi, Sheridan. Like what?" Nathan asked.

"Well, the cuts on her body look like they were made post-mortem, which is different from Jordan. His cuts displayed lesions caused by haemorrhaging, suggesting they were made before the killer stabbed him in the heart. Also, we can't see any kind of puncture wound on her suggesting an injection. The autopsy will tell us more, though."

"And these markings on the wall?" Kate asked.

"Similar to the marks we found carved into the tree that Jordan was hung from," Sheridan explained. "The word, 'today' is new though."

"We know where that fits in," Nathan replied, but didn't explain himself.

Sheridan looked to Nathan for a moment, as if expecting him to elaborate, but then shrugged and looked away when it was clear he wouldn't.

"Well, this certainly looks like our man," Nathan suggested, looking over at Kate.

She nodded. "He's adapted to the circumstances of the location, but the MO certainly seems the same. I bet he killed her first to keep her quiet while he went to work with the cuts and marks. She'd have screamed the place down otherwise."

"And put up a fight," Nathan added.

"That too," Kate agreed. "No photo though."

"No..." Nathan answered, looking a little unsure what that might mean.

"Was he having us on, showing us photos of Mark? Was Naomi always the intended victim, or did he change his mind?"

"No idea. Alright, let's go meet this witness," Nathan said and allowed the sergeant to lead them out.

After removing the forensic suits, they were shown over to the witness who sat in the back of a nearby van being comforted by a female officer. Nathan nudged Kate forward, urging her to take the lead.

"Hi," Kate said, checking her notes as the woman looked up. "Abby Whickham, isn't it?"

"Yeah," Abby said with a nod. Her red, bloodshot eyes suggested she'd been crying.

"I'm DC O'Connell, and this is DS Halliwell. We'd like to ask you a few questions, if that's okay?"

Abby nodded but remained quiet.

"I understand you saw Naomi arguing with her former husband earlier tonight. Is that right?" Kate asked.

Abby nodded again. "They were out front shouting at each other. Steve was upset, yelling at her. He's been bothering her for a while, but this was the first time he turned up here."

"He'd not been here before?"

Abby shook her head. "Naomi had kept her new home address secret from him. She'd been really careful about it too."

"But he knew where she worked," Kate pressed.

"I think so, yes. He'd seen her in town a few times recently. Followed her around, hurled abuse at her, that kind of thing."

"But he didn't follow her home?"

"She drove home from work. As far as we know, Steve doesn't have a car."

"So somehow, he found out where Naomi lived."

"Or someone told him," Nathan added.

Kate nodded in agreement. "So, tell me about the argument, how did it end?"

"I heard them at first and looked out the window. When I saw it was Naomi, I rushed out to help her. I brought her inside, away from him. I locked the outer door, so he couldn't get in. I stayed with her for a while. She told me about the interview she'd had with you lot."

"We had a few questions for her," Kate replied, having noticed the accusatory tone in Abby's voice.

"Mm-hmm. She told me she got the impression that you thought she was involved in Jordan's death."

"We have to look at things from all angles," Kate replied. "So, when was the last time you saw her alive?"

"When she went back to her apartment. It was late. I offered to let her stay at my place, but she wanted to sleep in her own bed. So, she left. That was at about eleven."

"And you didn't hear anything at all the rest of the night?"

"No. I went to bed after she left, but I woke up early for work. I wanted to check she was okay so I gave her a call. When she didn't answer I went to knock on her door."

"And she didn't answer," Kate suggested.

"No. Actually, the door was ajar, so I went inside. That's when I found... You know..."

"I see," Kate said. "Have you met Steve before? Did you know it was Steve when you saw him out the window?"

"I've seen pictures, but Naomi was shouting his name anyway. I knew who it was."

"Can you give us a description? Is this the man?" She asked, holding up her phone with his photo on the screen.

"That's him. But he doesn't look like that anymore. He's a mess. Long hair, beard. He stinks too. He looks like some kind of tramp."

"Okay, thank you," Kate said, slipping her phone back into her pocket. "So, how do you know Naomi, apart from being neighbours?"

"We were in the women's shelter at the same time. We just got to know each other, had similar stories with our ex's. You know?" Abby glanced up at Nathan with a cold expression on her face. Did she hate all men? Kate wondered.

"And you both moved here?" Kate asked.

Abby nodded. "Everyone in this building is from the shelter."

Kate nodded. "Okay, thank you. I think that's all for now. You've been very helpful."

"Thanks," Nathan added.

Abby nodded to them, and they left her with the female officer.

"So, Steve found out where she lived, came here late last night, confronted Naomi, and had an argument with her," Nathan summarised. "Only for her to be found murdered the next day."

"We really need to find Steve," Kate said, "It's not looking good for him."

"No, it's not," he said as they made their way back towards their car.

Sergeant Dyson stepped up to them. "Do you have everything you need?"

"I think so," Kate said.

"Are there any CCTV on the premises?" Nathan asked, and Kate kicked herself for forgetting to check that.

"No, none," the sergeant replied.

Kate frowned. "Isn't that a bit of an oversight, given all these residents are from abusive relationships?"

Sergeant Dyson shrugged. "I can look into it for you, if you like?"

"That would be great," she said with a smile, and the pair renewed their walk towards their vehicle. "Let's ask if we can get a statement out to the press as well, reiterating our desire to find Steve," Kate said.

Nathan nodded. "I'll suggest it."

CHAPTER 23

"So, are you going to tell me?" Nathan asked as they drove east out of Guildford, heading back to the station.

"Hmm? Tell you what?" Kate asked, feeling a little confused as he broke her train of thought.

"About what happened in there. This is the second time you've had a funny turn upon seeing a dead body. I mean, are you squeamish? Is this going to become an issue?" Nathan pressed.

Kate sighed. She'd hoped he'd not noticed, but if this was going to affect her, she guessed she'd need to explain herself at some point. Still, she wasn't sure she was totally comfortable confiding in him.

"It's nothing. It's just some early nerves, you know. First case, and all that?"

"No, it's not. Come on, what's really going on here?"

"Look, I told you, it's…"

"Don't you trust me?" he asked, cutting her off.

"Well, yes…" It actually didn't feel like a lie, which surprised her.

"Then tell me."

She shifted in her seat, feeling very uncomfortable, but she also knew that this was not going to go away.

"Kate?" Nathan pushed again.

"Alright, okay. It's not the sight of a dead body. I'm not squeamish like that. It's something else. It's…" She sighed. "When I was a teenager, just sixteen, my aunt was found murdered. Killed, in the middle of a stone circle. It was a ritual killing. She was sacrificed." That was all he needed to know, she thought, looking away from him. She stared out of her window as the flashes of memory rippled through her mind. She remembered Cork and the events that took place there, but there was no need for him to know about that.

Some things were best left buried in the past.

"Ah, I see."

"This happened in Ireland, just outside Cork. They thought it was Satanists or something."

"Were you close to your aunt?"

Kate nodded. "Yeah. I was. She was like an older sister to me. I guess these killings are just bringing old memories to the surface."

"You don't have to do this, you know. If this is too close to home for you, you can request a different case. A different partner."

"No!" she barked in reply.

Nathan gave her a look of surprise at her outburst.

"I mean. I'd rather stay on the case if it's all the same."

"Are you sure?" Nathan asked.

Kate nodded. "My aunt, Fiona, her killer was never caught. I made a promise to her that I would strive to make sure that the same injustice didn't happen to anyone else. After her death, I knew I wanted to be a detective. I wanted to hunt down killers like hers and bring them to justice. Don't take me off this case. Please. I need to see this through. I need to find this killer."

"Are you sure you can handle it?"

Kate nodded, feeling that steely resolve deep inside her that drove her onwards. "I'll handle it. You have my word."

"As long as you're sure."

"I am," she replied.

"Okay. Thank you for telling me, by the way. I had no idea."

"It's fine. I knew it would come out eventually. It's probably better that you know. It might help me deal with it better."

"Is there anything I can do to help?"

She nodded. "Not really. Not unless you can find my aunt's killer?"

"Well, not right now," Nathan answered lightly. "Maybe this afternoon?"

Kate laughed. "Alright, so how are we going to find Steve? We really need to bring him in. Naomi said she thought he was homeless."

Nathan nodded his agreement. "Well, either he's sleeping rough, or in a squat somewhere."

"Abby confirmed the unkempt look that Steve has now. Long hair, beard... It sounds like he's living rough and hasn't got two pennies to rub together."

"I've already got a few uniforms checking through some of the known squats. We should maybe have a look in some abandoned buildings as well. Anywhere people can find shelter and get some rest."

"We have a list of places like that then?"

"We do. It's not exhaustive, but there's a lot of them. If nothing else comes up from the forensics or any CCTV, it might be something we need to try. We could do some today. Start asking some questions."

"Someone might know something," she agreed.

"You never know," Nathan replied as he pulled the car into the station car park and brought it to a stop.

Kate climbed out of the car. At least going around to the squats and abandoned buildings was something to do. She'd much rather be out there, driving around, speaking to people, investigating, and trying to find Steve than be sat at her computer doing paperwork.

There was a small mountain of that to do as well, of course. But that was the nature of the job. She sighed to herself as she and Nathan marched into the front entrance of the station.

The press was still there and tried to get the usual comments from them, but they pushed on through, ignoring them as they entered the building.

"Ugh," she said as the door closed behind them. "We need to look at getting them off the premises, I do not want to deal with that every day."

"I hear ya," Nathan said as they crossed reception. Kate looked up to see a dishevelled looking man who'd been sat down, get up from his seat. He was staring at her with a curious expression on his face.

"Hey, you that detective off the TV?"

Kate raised her eyebrows and then smiled. "I spoke to some reporters yesterday, yes. Can I help you?"

"Yeh on that case, right? The dead Estate Agent?"

Kate nodded.

"I know where your man is," he said.

"My man?"

"Yeh lookin' for 'im. Steve, right?"

Kate moved a little closer to the man, followed by Nathan, and lowered her voice. "You know where he is?"

The man smiled and shifted his weight back. He crossed his arms, looking smug. "I might do."

"Well, do you or don't you?" Nathan asked, his voice steely.

"Depends, don' it."

"On what?" Kate asked.

"What yeh gonna' do feh me?"

"What we're going to do for you?"

"How bad do yeh want that information, like?" He said with a shrug. "Cos I know where he is, like. I can send yeh right to 'im."

"Is that right?" Nathan asked. "How do we know you're not just some nutjob who's seen Detective O'Connell on the news and thinks he can make a quick buck, or even just get some attention by coming down here and spinning some lies?"

"That's up to you, like, innit? Believe me or don'. But I's tellin' yehs, I know where he is." The man then clamped his mouth shut and gave Kate the impression he was basically saying the ball was in their court.

Kate turned to look at Nathan. He looked back at her, his eyes narrowed, clearly weighing up the options.

"Alright, come with us," he said beckoning the man forward. Kate walked after him, wondering where Nathan was going to go with this and followed him to the reception desk where he signed in and got checked over for weapons or anything else dangerous.

Leading the man through a door, Nathan directed him into one of the interview rooms and gestured for him to sit. Nathan stayed standing, and Kate took her place beside him.

"What do you want then, Jimmy?" Nathan asked, using the name the man had given when he'd signed in.

Jimmy smiled. "A reward."

"You mean money?"

"I think this information is valuable. I reckon I deserve a reward, like. Don' yeh think? I mean, I could go to the press."

Nathan stared at the man as if he were something stuck to the bottom of his shoe. Kate watched him chew on his cheek for a moment, and then turn and make for the door. "Kate," he said.

She followed him out.

"What do you think?" Nathan asked after he closed the door.

"I'm not sure. I don't know if I believe him or not. If there was some way of verifying that he really does know Steve, then maybe I'd be happy digging into my wallet."

Nathan nodded. "Yep. I'm reluctant to let him go without getting the information from him, though. If he really does know where

Steve is, and we don't try to follow this up, then we're up shit creek if Steve is the killer, and kills again."

"Negligence," Kate muttered.

"Right," Nathan replied. "Okay, let's see if we can find anything out."

Kate followed him back into the room. This time Nathan sat in one of the seats facing Jimmy, and Kate took the one beside him as he began to talk.

"Alright, we're interested, but need to kn-"

"I want to speak to her," Jimmy interrupted him.

"What?" Nathan asked.

"I don't want to speak to you. I want to speak to her. Kate. Right?"

Kate got a sinking feeling as a shiver rippled up her back. That was a little creepy, but maybe she could turn this to her advantage.

"Alright," Kate replied. "You can talk to me."

"Good," Jimmy said with a smug grin.

"But as Detective Halliwell was saying, we need a little more than just your say so, that you know who Steve is."

"Alright. Well, I know the fellah. So, ask me a question."

"What's his wife's name?" Kate asked.

Jimmy smiled. "Ex-wife, you mean."

Kate smiled back. "Ex-wife," Kate corrected herself.

"Naomi. An' he ended up on the street when his restaurant went tits up, like."

Kate looked over at Nathan, who nodded to her, apparently satisfied.

She sighed and pulled the small wallet she usually carried in her jacket from the inside pocket and folded out the three notes that were in there. Nathan did likewise and handed her the money. It wasn't much. It was just over fifty quid, but she hoped it was enough. She held it up before her.

"Will this be enough?"

"Aye, it will, like," he said reaching across for it.

Kate pulled it away. "The info."

Jimmy's eyes flicked between her and the money, clearly suspicious. "Gimme half before, and half after."

Kate thought about it and then pulled two of the notes out. She handed them to him. "You can have twenty now, the rest when we're satisfied with the information."

Jimmy hungrily stuffed the notes into his pocket, and stared at the remaining money in her hand, apparently wrestling with himself.

"Okay. Alright," he said and recited an address to them that both she and Nathan copied down. "He's there right now."

Kate knew roughly where the address was in Guildford and it wasn't too far away. Still, she eyed the information suspiciously and looked back at Jimmy. "You're sure about this?"

"Positive," he said, holding his hand out for the rest of the money.

Kate looked over at Nathan, who shrugged and then nodded.

Kate handed Jimmy the cash, who snatched it from her hand and counted it quickly. Apparently pleased, he stood up.

"Thank you very much, it's been a pleasure doing business with you."

A short while later, they stood in the corridor outside the interview room, watching the uniformed officer show Jimmy out.

"Do we check this out?" Kate asked.

"Absolutely," Nathan replied as they spotted DCI Dean enter the corridor and approach them.

"There you are. What are you doing down here? There's been another killing, you know."

"Sorry sir, we had a walk-in with some information."

"Oh, and?"

"We have a lead on the whereabouts of Steve Brewster, our main suspect. The walk-in gave us an address. A disused building that's being used as a squat."

"Was he credible?"

"Very," Nathan replied. "He knew details of Steve's life that a stranger would not know."

"Then what are you waiting for? Leave the details in my office, get out there and bring him in."

Nathan nodded. "Okay, good. I'd like some uniform backup on this," he said.

"I'll get a couple of officers to meet you out front, now go!"

CHAPTER 24

After a quick visit upstairs to the office to make sure they had everything they needed, leaving the details of the interview with Jimmy on the DCI's desk, they headed outside to find a marked car with two officers inside, waiting to follow them. Kate jumped into Nathan's car, and within moments they were away, speeding into Guildford, making for one of the parades of shops just out from the centre of town.

"I hope this isn't a wild goose chase," Kate said as they drove in.

"The walk-in seemed genuine enough. I'm hopeful," Nathan replied.

Kate nodded. "So, what's the plan?"

"I'm not sure. Depends on what the property looks like. If there's only one entrance, we'll head in as one unit, but if we have a front and rear entrance, we might need to head inside in pairs. Two in the front and two in the back."

"Sounds like a plan," Kate replied, preparing herself for what was to come. Entering somewhere where the police were not welcome always got the adrenaline pumping. She'd been involved in a few of these kinds of raids while in uniform, and they were often dramatic affairs.

As they approached the property, they turned off their sirens and lights to avoid spooking the squatters and pulled over about fifteen metres up the road. Kate jumped out, ran around to the boot of the car and opened it up. She pulled out one of the black stab vests that were inside, pulled it on over her head and grabbed a baton as well. Nathan joined her and did the same.

Within moments, they were hustling up the pavement, approaching the squat. The building they needed to enter had clearly been disused for a while. Its downstairs windows were boarded up, with graffiti all over the walls. There was a six foot, double gate on the side closest to them. A loose chain secured it but allowed a gap big enough for someone to easily slip through. Ahead, beyond the gate, the front door led straight onto the path, but they couldn't see it clearly from where they were, tucked up against the wall to try and keep from being spotted.

Nathan, who had taken point, assessed the building and turned to address them.

"You three, stay here, I'll check the front entrance," he said, and jogged along, past the gate, and up to the front door. Kate watched him check it, pulling on the boarding with little effect, and then jog back.

"Shut fast, they must get in through the back," he said, jabbing his thumb in the direction of the gate. "Come on."

Nathan led them through the gap in the gate, into a sizable yard area, filled with overgrown weeds embedded in the cracked concrete, or taking over areas of hard packed mud. Rubbish and debris were dumped everywhere, but several pathways had been cleared through the mess to the gate and a back wall with some boxes piled up next to it. To their right, the dilapidated building loomed above them, with a single entrance leading into it.

Kate felt a rush of both excitement and fear as she looked at the property, and steeled her nerves against the urge to flee the potential danger.

Nathan led them forward, threading them through the yard and up to the doorway, which sat slightly ajar. He turned to Kate and the two officers behind her.

"Ready?" he whispered.

Kate nodded and saw the two backup officers do the same.

"Good. You come with me, you stick with Kate," Nathan directed them. "Kate, go left, I'll go right."

Nate shoulder barged the door and rushed inside.

"Police! Show yourselves." He yelled as he moved inside. Kate followed. Nathan lunged to the right, towards the front of the house.

Kate moved left through another doorway and found herself in the kitchen.

"Police," she shouted as she moved, only to find a young woman sat at the table, her arms raised in surrender.

"I ain't done nuthin'," the girl called out.

"Steve. I'm looking for Steve," she said to her.

The girl shrugged. Kate hadn't expected cooperation and moved on through the room to the far door.

"Police," Kate called out as she entered the next room, only to be tackled from her right. She was thrown against the wall with a thud that rattled her skeleton.

"Piss off, filth," the man yelled as he pushed her up against the wall.

Kate grunted as she swung her baton and caught him in the ribs. He made a pained noise, only to have a tall, strong man in police-black smash into his side and throw him off her.

Kate's legs went wobbly for a moment as she caught her breath and sank into a crouch.

The attacker yelled in pain as he hit a table that stood in the middle of the dirty room, and fell off it. Detritus was everywhere. Empty food cartons, rubbish bags, boxes, and all kinds of drug paraphernalia scattered over the table and floor.

"You won't kick us out. You can't. This is private property," the attacker muttered, clutching his ribs.

Kate stood back up and walked over as she heard Nathan breach another room on the other side of the house.

"I don't want to kick you out. I just want to find Steve," Kate said.

"Steve?" the man said, sounding confused.

"Is he here? We need to speak to him."

Kate watched the man's eye flick to look upstairs, and then sideways as he considered his answer.

"Umm..." he prevaricated.

"Upstairs, yeah?" Kate cut him off. The man's eyes went as wide as plates. Gotcha, she thought and smiled smugly at him.

"Er, no. He's not up there," but he sounded desperate.

"Then you won't mind us taking a look, right?" Kate said and began to make her way across the house towards the front door, where she guessed the main staircase was.

Walking out through another door, Kate found herself in a reception area at the front of the building, with a staircase leading up to the next floor. Nathan strode out of another room on her right.

"Any trouble?" he asked.

"Nothing we couldn't handle," Kate replied as they reached the foot of the stairs.

Looking up, a man with a beard was five steps down from the top, frozen in place, as if scared to move. The moment Kate looked up at him, his eyes bugged.

"Shit," he hissed under his breath and bolted back up the stairs.

Nathan was after him the next second, charging up the stairs, taking three at a time. "Steve Brewster? It's the Police, stay where you are," he shouted as he ran.

Kate followed, their shoes banging on the bare wooden steps as they ran.

Steve dodged left and tried to shut a door on Nathan, but he got a foot in the door and rammed it with his shoulder. It slammed open, hitting the wall with a bang as Nathan barged through. Kate reached the landing and glanced around, checking no one was moving to interfere.

She couldn't see anyone and followed Nathan into the room. Her partner had knocked the man with the beard to the floor, but he was struggling against Nathan's grip. Kate moved to Nathan's side and helped him wrestle the man's arms into a pair of cuffs.

As they clicked home, the fight seemed to drain out of the man, and he relaxed on the floor as one of the other officers who'd accompanied them, appeared in the doorway.

"Everything alright?" he asked.

"Yeah, we got it," Kate replied, and moved to get a better look at the man. She recognised his features, even with all the ragged facial hair. "It's Steve, right?" Kate asked.

"Who wants to know?"

"Steve Brewster," Nathan said. "We're arresting you under suspicion of the murder of Jordan Donaldson and Naomi Sawyer. You do not-"

"What? Naomi? What's happened to Naomi?"

"Steve, you do n-"

"What's happened to Naomi?" Steve yelled, his voice cracking from the emotion in it.

"She's dead, Steve. Murdered."

"No. No, that's not true. No. That can't be true. I saw her last night. She was fine."

"You argued with her last night. Fought with her," Kate pressed.

"Yeah, I know. But I didn't hurt her. How can she be dead? You must be mistaken."

"I wish we were," Kate muttered.

Steve seemed to withdraw into himself then, muttering under his breath in somewhat incoherent ramblings as Nathan finally managed to recite the Police Caution without being interrupted.

Nathan then hauled him up with Kate's help, pulling him to his feet as he continued to mutter to himself. They got him out of the house and into the marked car without further trouble, and they set off back in convoy.

"He didn't seem to know that Naomi had been killed," Kate said as they set off, this time following the marked car out of the city.

"Hmm," Nathan answered her.

Kate frowned, wondering what this meant for their investigation, providing that Steve wasn't putting on an act to try and throw them off the scent. It wouldn't be the first time that someone had put on an Oscar-winning performance to try and escape justice.

She knew she had to be careful though, and not get too focused in on one suspect to the exclusion of all others, despite the evidence against him.

"Are we barking up the wrong tree here?"

"I don't know, but that was a hell of a reaction to the news of her death," he said, shaking his head. "I have a bad feeling about this."

Kate agreed. "I know what you mean."

Back at the station, they took him in through the custody suite and booked him into one of their holding cells before retreating back upstairs to the Murder Team's main office.

"So, what do we have?" DI Mason asked as they entered the office. He'd walked over with a curious smile. "Some kind of homeless mastermind? A crime of passion by the victim's former husband? Not much of a conspiracy there," Sam smirked.

"We don't know he did it yet, sir" Kate replied, as Nathan seemed to bite his tongue to keep from saying something stupid.

"Of course. Well, if you find out he's part of some kind of knightly order or something, be sure to let me know, yeah?"

Kate didn't find his comments amusing and cocked an eyebrow at him. Nearby, DS Taylor laughed at his partner's wit. Nathan had already walked off, making his way back to his desk.

"Was it something I said?" DI Mason asked no one in particular, looking hurt, before laughing again.

Kate rolled her eyes as she crossed the room to her desk. "Ignore them," she said as she sat down.

"I'm used to it. They're idiots."

"Yeah. They are. They don't know what they're talking about."

"Hmmm," Nathan replied half-heartedly. "You didn't seem too convinced with my theories the other day either."

Kate paused and gave Nathan a little side eye. She cleared her throat as she thought through her response to him. "Well, it was a lot to take in, to be honest. I'm not saying I don't believe you, I'm just saying, give me time, and proof."

Nathan nodded to her as he watched her through narrowed eyes.

She wasn't lying to him, but she was far from convinced of his ideas about there being some kind of secret group behind these killings. Also, with the way this case was turning out, it felt more like some kind of crime of passion than anything else.

Steve had put on quite the show back at the house and seemed genuinely shocked that Naomi was dead. But that was a reaction he could have practised, along with an alibi or story that he might have cooked up between last night and now.

"Alright, let's pull together our evidence and work out what we're going to ask him."

Kate nodded, and turned to her desk, still slightly distracted by the comments Nathan had just voiced. They were ready within the hour and only had to wait a short time for Steve to be finished speaking with his appointed duty solicitor before they could head downstairs.

"Do you want me to take the lead again?" she asked.

"We'll share it," Nathan said as they approached the room. Kate nodded and followed Nathan inside, where Steve sat with his solicitor.

Kate set the DIR to record, and joined Nathan at the table, opposite Steve and his legal counsel. Nathan let Kate run through the necessary info for the recording, stating everyone's name and making sure that Steve knew he was still under caution before they proceeded. Kate noted the look on Steve's face as he sat and watched her run through the procedure. He looked fed up and somewhat defeated by what had been going on.

Again, she began to doubt that he was the killer they were looking for, but repeated to herself that she needed to keep an open mind and realise that it was in his interest to avoid being charged with Naomi's murder.

"Tell me about your relationship with Naomi Sawyer," Nathan asked once Kate was finished.

"She was my wife," Steve said.

"But she isn't any longer?"

"We're divorced," he admitted.

"And why is that?" Nathan continued.

"We broke up. She left me."

"Why did she leave you, Mr Brewster?" Nathan pressed.

"I guess we weren't suited to each other," he said with a shrug.

"And...?"

"And what?" Steve asked. He appeared genuinely confused by Nathan's question, even though it was painfully obvious to Kate what he was getting at.

"Naomi reported that you were violent towards her, correct?"

"Yeah, she did," Steve answered, a note of resignation in his voice.

"You hit her, didn't you?"

Steve nodded.

"You hurt her."

"I wouldn't kill her," Steve answered, clearly seeing where Nathan was going with this.

"Really? Now, why don't I believe you?"

"I don't know. But I wouldn't. I love her. I couldn't kill her."

"But you could hit her," Kate said, cutting in for the first time.

Steve turned to her, apparently a little surprised by her outburst. "I don't mean to. I just get angry, you know? I don't want to hurt her."

"But you can't stop yourself?"

"No. I mean, yeah, I can. I just…"

"You just what?" Kate asked.

"I lash out sometimes. I hate myself for doing it. But I couldn't kill her. I couldn't kill anyone."

"How can we believe you?" Nathan asked. "If you can't control yourself, then maybe you couldn't control yourself last night."

"No…"

"Where were you last night, Steve?" Kate asked.

"Home. I was at home."

"Was that before or after you had your argument with Naomi at her flat?"

"Err, be-. I mean, both. But how do you…?"

"How do we know you were at Naomi's last night? Because you were seen, Mr Brewster."

Kate saw the dawning realisation of understanding as he apparently realised who'd seen him. "Oh," he said.

"That's right. So, you, her ex-husband with violent tendencies had a fight outside her flat last night, only for her to be discovered murdered this morning. You see how this looks, right?"

"But I didn't do it..."

"How did you know where Naomi lived?" Kate asked. "Did you follow her home from somewhere?"

"No, I was tol-" He stopped then, and stared into the middle distance for a moment, frowning slightly as his mind worked. "I was told. I've been set up."

"Told? By whom?"

"That bastard," Steve said, his voice like cold steel.

"Who are you talking about?" Kate asked, getting a tingling sensation up her spine suddenly, as she got the feeling that they were onto something.

Steve took a couple of beats to himself, and then looked up at them. "Look, I know I've been violent towards Naomi, and no one regrets that more than I do. But you have to believe me when I say I would never kill her. I've not been violent towards her for months now."

"So you say," Kate answered him.

"Yes, I do say, but anyway. Like I was saying. I didn't kill Naomi, but I think I know who did, or, who might have anyway."

"Go on," Nathan said.

"Wilson Hollins," Steve replied with a hint of gravitas in his voice.

Kate raised an eyebrow and caught a glimpse of Nathan's slightly surprised look. "You mean the property developer?"

"The one who owns Jordan Donaldson's office?" Nathan asked.

"That's him. He told me where Naomi was living."

"He told you?" Nathan said.

"That's right, but that's not all. Shit, I knew he was up to something, but I never... Ugh," he said, shaking his head.

"What's up?"

"Look, I've seen him at that office, where Naomi works. I've seen him there, but I've known him for a long time. He looks different, though. Hardly recognised him at first, but it's certainly him. I know it is. He's changed his name too."

"What are you talking about?" Nathan asked.

"He was at school with us. Wilson went to the same school as me and Jordan, but he was called Gary back then. He was always a bit of a weird one. He was bullied a lot, you know. Jordan and Naomi were terrible. Cruel, really."

"But Naomi went to a different school," Kate countered, but in her mind, the puzzle pieces were falling into place, and she could feel the adrenaline starting to pump through her system.

"Yeah," Steve replied. But we still saw each other outside of school. It was at its worst when Jordan and Naomi were going out. They humiliated him."

"So, Jordan and Naomi were at school with Wilson, and you?" Kate asked.

Steve nodded. "They used to wait for him outside of school and follow him around, call him names, hit him. You know, the usual. I didn't see most of it, but I heard about it."

"So, how did you first meet up with Wilson?" Nathan asked.

He found me outside the Estate Agents a while back," Steve said with a sigh. "I'd been following Naomi. I'd seen her working for Jordan and remembered their relationship from back in school. I was jealous. I couldn't help it. I had to make sure she was alright. Anyway, he just kind of bumped into me. I didn't recognise him at first. He's not the scrawny wimp he once was. Maybe Jordan wasn't aware of who Wilson was. I figured it out a little while ago, but kept it to myself."

"You mean to say, you didn't recognise an old school friend?"

"He's changed. Wilson doesn't look like he did back then. He was a bit of a dork and a loner with messy hair and glasses. Skinny too. He had terrible acne. I mean, there was a resemblance there, for sure, but it wasn't obvious at all. Have you seen him? He's tall, muscled, bald, and I'm guessing he wears contacts now. The name change threw me, too. Anyway, he told me yesterday where Naomi was living now. So, I went to have a look."

"I take it she didn't like you knowing where she lived?" Kate asked.

"No, not really," Steve replied unhappily. "Look, you have to believe me. I know it was him. Why else would he tell me where Naomi lived?"

As he spoke, a thought suddenly occurred to Kate. She pulled out her phone and quickly found a webpage with the correct news report on it with a photo of the victim.

"What's up?" Nathan asked her.

"One moment," Kate answered. "I want to check something." She made the image fill the screen and showed it to Steve. "Do you recognise this man?"

"Err, oh, yeah. He was at the same school as me and Jordan. A year or so older, though. He was another one who bullied Wilson."

Kate smiled and turned her phone to Nathan.

"Mark Summers," Nathan muttered.

"That's him, that's his name," Steve replied. "Yeah, he and some of his mates picked on Wilson as well. Mark was bad, though. He used to beat him up. Piece of work, that one."

Nathan's eyes flicked between her and her phone, and then he nodded. Kate put the phone away as Nathan stood up. "Thank you for your time, Mr Brewster, but we're going to have to cut this interview short. We'll be back to talk to you again shortly, mind."

Kate got up and nodded to Steve before following Nathan out of the interview room. He was moving quickly, but she caught him up.

"Are we going after Wilson Hollins?" Kate asked.

"Damn right we are," Nathan muttered. "I have some questions I want to ask him."

CHAPTER 25

"Do you think he's telling the truth?" Kate asked, as they sped into the outskirts of Guildford, blues and twos going to clear the way and get there as quick as they could.

Nathan nodded. "I think so. It all fits."

"How did he do it, though?" Kate asked. "How did he kidnap and kill Jordan?"

"He's the owner of the building, so I'm guessing he has a key and just let himself in. He'd probably already taken Jordan by the time Naomi got there that night. Why, don't you believe him?"

"No, I do. I was playing devil's advocate. Like you say, it all feels right."

"Doesn't quite fit with the family man image he presented to us, though, does it?"

"I bet he's leading a double life," Kate suggested, as memories of stories she'd read came back to her about Mobsters who were violent serial murderers, but also doting fathers.

Was Wilson, or Gary, the same kind of man?

"Probably. I'd put money on his wife having no idea about all this, if it's true," Nathan agreed.

Kate sighed. "Shit, that poor kid. That's horrendous."

"Nothing we can do. We'll tread carefully, though. No need to cause too much upset if we can avoid it."

"Yeah," Kate agreed, thinking troubling thoughts as she stared out the window. She hated it when innocent parties were caught up in the actions of one of these criminals and had their lives shattered when the truth came to light.

There was nothing for it, though. They had broken the law, and more innocent lives would be at risk if they delayed.

Turning the siren off a couple of streets before they reached the Hollins' household, they soon pulled up outside Wilson's attractive home and made their way up to the front gate, and the intercom that was beside it.

Nathan pressed the buzzer, and a moment later, a female voice sounded from the speaker.

"Hello?"

Nathan looked a little surprised. "Hi. Sorry, it's Detectives Kate O'Connell and Nathan Halliwell here to see Wilson Hollins?"

"Oh. Well sure, come in," the voice answered. Moments later, the gates parted, allowing them into the driveway where they parked. An attractive woman in her mid-thirties stood waiting for them at the door, her sandy blonde hair falling loosely over her shoulders. The little girl they had met on their previous visit hugged her leg, looking up at them as they walked from the car. She caught Kate's eye and smiled. Kate returned the expression but knew it probably looked a little fake, not that the girl would pick up on that subtlety.

"They're police people, mommy," the girl said as they crossed the last few metres towards the door.

"I know sweetheart."

"Secret police people. They're good at hiding."

"Is that right? Hi, I'm Mary, Wilson's wife. I don't think we met before."

"No, we haven't. Nice to meet you," Kate replied.

"Hi," Nathan said.

"I'm afraid Wilson isn't here right now. He's at work. Can I help you with anything?"

"We need to speak to Wilson urgently regarding the investigation into Jordan Donaldson's murder. We have some questions to ask him," Kate explained, sensing that Nathan wanted her to take the lead in dealing with Mary.

"Well, he should be at his office," Mary answered.

"You're sure he's not here?" Nathan asked. Kate could hear the suspicious tone in his voice and wondered if Mary had picked up on it.

Mary frowned at him. "Quite sure," she replied defensively. She'd noticed it, Kate thought.

"Do you mind if we confirm that for ourselves?" Nathan pressed.

"Sorry, Mrs Hollins, but this really is quite urgent, and we need to be sure," Kate added in an attempt to keep her calm.

Mary looked between both of them, clearly very suspicious about what this was all about. She shrugged. "Sure, go ahead," she said.

"Wait here," Nathan said, and moved quickly inside. Kate watched him go, and looked up at Mrs Hollins, giving her a tense smile.

"What is this all about?" Mary asked.

"I'm sorry, but we're really not at liberty to say. The investigation is still ongoing, and we really can't discuss it."

"Is daddy in trouble?" the girl asked.

"No, Daisy. Everything's fine, don't worry," Mary said to her daughter.

Part of Kate hoped Steve was lying if only to save Daisy from the heartbreak that would follow if Wilson turned out to be the man that Steve said he was.

"He's not, is he? In any trouble, I mean?" Mary asked her as if sensing the tension in Kate's body.

"We just need to speak to him, that's all," Kate answered, hoping that nothing in her body language gave anything away. She felt like she was broadcasting half-truths and subterfuge for all to see as she stood there, doing her best to keep a calm and composed demeanour.

Mary nodded, giving Kate a half smile, but there wasn't any warmth in it at all.

"Do you mind me asking where Wilson was last night?"

"Working late," Mary replied. "He was out early again today. He works incredibly hard to provide for this family, you know. We only live here because of his dedication to his work."

Kate gave Mary a half-hearted smile. "And can anyone confirm that he was working late?"

"His secretary," Mary suggested. "She'll be at his office today as well."

"Okay, thank you," Kate replied.

Moments later, Nathan stepped back outside with a nod. "So, he's at his office, is he?" Kate asked.

"That's right," Mary replied, still clearly suspicious as she recited the address.

Kate wrote it down and then eyed the top line on her notepad and glanced up at Nathan, who met her gaze. He didn't need to say anything. He was clearly thinking the same thing she was on finding out where Wilson's office was located.

"Thank you, Mrs Hollins, you've been most helpful," Kate said as they walked off the property and returned to their car in silence.

The instant both doors had closed, Kate turned to Nathan. "I'm right, aren't I? That address is just around the corner from the Estate Agents, isn't it?"

Nathan nodded. "In the same parade of shops, yeah."

"Shit. We should have picked up on that earlier," Kate answered as Nathan gunned the engine, and they accelerated away from Wilson's home.

"Maybe," Nathan replied, half agreeing with her.

"Mary said that Wilson was working late last night," Kate said.

"Makes sense. Killing someone is a lot of work."

Kate let her eyebrows bob up and down. "Know that from experience, do you?"

"Didn't you know? I'm the Guildford strangler," Nathan joked.

"I thought there was something odd about you," Kate replied.

"Well, now you know."

They drove into town and parked illegally a short distance from the office. Nathan popped a police ID card in the front window, and they both got out.

"It's up there," Nathan said, pointing to an office above a nearby shop.

"Hang on," Kate said and started up the street towards the corner, two shops up. "I wanna check something."

"What?" Nathan asked following along behind her.

Fifteen metres later, Kate stood on the corner and looked along the road up to where the Estate Agents was located towards the far end of this parade of shops. "It's close," Kate commented. Nathan stepped up beside her and silently agreed.

"Too close. Come on," Nathan said and led her back towards the door that led up to the office. As he reached it, he paused, looking up the road. He then walked up past the office to a cut-through between two other stores, to a loading area at the back. He looked at Kate with a raised eyebrow.

"I'll put money on this linking up with the loading area behind the Estate Agents," Kate said.

"Let's find out," Nathan said and walked up it. Sure enough, the loading area, which was maybe three car widths across, followed the parade of shops around and linked up to the area behind the Estate Agents.

"So, we now have means to add to opportunity and motive," Kate stated as they moved back to the office door, and scanned over the intercom unit on the wall.

Nathan stabbed the button beside the Hollins Holdings Ltd label and held it until the speaker clicked, and a digitised female voice sounded through it.

"Hello, can I help you?"

Nathan held his warrant card up for the tiny camera set into the intercom unit. "DC's Halliwell and O'Connell, can we speak to you please?"

"Oh, sure. Come in," the voice answered, and the door unlocked. Nathan wasted no time in stomping up the steps, and Kate followed behind. She spotted the striking blonde girl stood in a doorway on the first floor, smiling brightly at them.

"Hi, come in," she said, sounding far happier than Kate thought she had any right to be and led them into the small, cosy office. Kate guessed this was Stacy Lee, Wilson's secretary who DC Arthur had spoken to for them the other day. Kate also got a certain impression from the girl, and about why Wilson might hire someone like her. She was young, maybe just into her twenties, and wore a very tight, fitted skirt and a blouse that could have done with having a few more buttons fastened on it. She was a beautiful young lady, that was for sure, and it made Kate wonder if Wilson had chosen her for her skills as a receptionist, or lack of those very same skills.

"Can I help you? I spoke to one of you detective people the day before yesterday."

"We know. We're looking for your boss, Wilson," Nathan said, looking around the room which housed a single desk with a computer on it. There were a couple of doors leading off from this room.

"Oh, well, he was here earlier. He's gone out though, to one of his commercial properties."

"Do you know which one?" Kate asked.

"Yep," she answered with a smile, apparently pleased with her answer and not elaborating further.

Kate gave her a look. "Can you tell us?"

"Oh, yes. Of course. Hold on, let me get the address," she said, turning to her desk and bending over to grab something off it. She bent at the waist, her skirt riding up and nearly showing off her underwear. Kate looked away before the girl mooned her, and spotted Nathan doing the same. Their eyes met, and Nathan rolled his eyes at her. Clearly, they were on the same wavelength on this.

Stacy stood up straight again and began riffling through an address book. "Hang on, I have it here somewhere."

"Were you working late with Wilson last night?" Kate asked while she waited.

"No," Stacy replied with a smile.

"But you were working late with Wilson on the seventh?"

Stacy paused and made a show of thinking about her question for a moment. "Erm, was that the night that Mr Donaldson was murdered?"

Kate nodded.

"Yes, I was here with Wilson. Terrible business all that. Can't believe that could happen here."

"And Wilson was in his office all night with you?"

"Oh yes," she replied. "I told the other one the same thing."

Nathan's eyes narrowed, Kate noticed. She turned to Stacy.

"He didn't leave the office at all?" Kate pressed. "He didn't step outside this door?"

"No. Oh, hmm. Hang on. Yes, he did. He went to the communal kitchen downstairs to get some food."

"Did you go with him?" Kate continued.

"No," the secretary answered brightly.

"How long was he gone?" Nathan asked.

"Oh, I don't know. Not long. Twenty minutes?"

"*Twenty minutes?*" Nathan asked, astounded.

"Around that. The microwave downstairs is a little iffy sometimes."

"Is it?" Nathan replied, deadpan.

"Well, Wilson says it is."

"Does he," Nathan added, his voice flat as he looked at Kate.

"You've never used it?" Kate asked.

"No. We have one in our kitchen, in there." Stacy pointed to one of the side doors in the room.

"Of course you do," Nathan answered. "Do you mind if we have a look around?"

"No, no, help yourselves. Can I get you a drink? Biscuit? I'm making myself one."

"Jammy Dodger?" Nathan replied as he moved to a nearby door and opened it up. Between them, they made short work of looking around the small office before returning to where they had been speaking to Stacy.

The blonde placed the biscuit tin on a table with a toothy smile, before returning to the kitchen to get her drink.

Nathan peered into the Tupperware box and raised an eyebrow. "Fig Rolls? The man's a monster."

"Oooh, I like those," Kate said and reached inside, pulling two of them out, much to Nathan's disgust.

"I don't think I know you anymore," he commented, as he reached in and removed a chocolate hobnob. "Now *this* is a biscuit," he said.

"These are too," Kate replied.

"No, Kate. Those are an abomination to God, and you'll do me the favour of keeping them away from me. Wouldn't want to get infected."

"Mmm," Kate replied, taking a bite from one and chewing it with her mouth open as she looked up at him.

"Vile creature," Nathan muttered, before Stacy returned, forcing them into an uncomfortable silence.

"Oh, I forgot. I found the address of the commercial property he's at while you were looking around. Here it is," she said, holding out the address book. "He goes there quite regularly."

"Does he? Have you been there?" Nathan replied.

"Oh, no. Never. I'm far too busy here," Stacy answered. "Anything else I can do for you?"

"Throw out the Fig Rolls before they breed," Nathan answered. "Otherwise, no. Thanks."

Stacy looked into the biscuit box with a confused frown.

"Ignore him," Kate answered. "We'll be in touch soon, I think."

"Okay, thank you," Stacy replied.

Back on the street, Kate finished her second Fig Roll and climbed into the car with Nathan as she thought about what they might find at this commercial property. "Why do I have a bad feeling about this?"

"Probably the two Fig Rolls you just ate," Nathan replied.

"At least I wasn't munching on a nob," she replied, eyebrow firmly raised.

"That's Hobnob to you. Chocolate one, too."

"Well, la-di-da," Kate replied.

Nathan smiled, and then the humour fell away from his face. He sighed. "I know what you mean, though. Come on, let's end this."

CHAPTER 26

"Hello?" Kate said down her phone, answering it as Nathan drove to the Hollins' commercial property.

"Kate, it's DC Rachel Arthur, I have some information you might be interested in," the Detective answered.

"Oh?" Kate answered.

"Have you got Wilson in custody yet?"

"Still trying to find him. What have you got for us?" she answered and tapped the speaker button so Nathan could hear as well.

"We've been doing some digging into Naomi's circumstances, where she lived, and who might have access to it, and we found something that we thought was interesting."

"Go on," Kate replied.

"Guess who owns the building that Naomi lived in?" Rachel asked.

"Let me guess, Wilson Hollins," Nathan answered.

"Hi, Nathan. Yeah, got it in one."

"Goddammit," Kate cursed. "He's been planning this for a long time."

"Looks that way. Good work, Rachel," Nathan answered.

"That's not all though," Rachel continued. "We thought we should check out what other buildings Wilson owns, and there was one other that got flagged up as interesting."

"Go on," Nathan answered.

"Yours Kate. He owns your building."

"Mine?" Kate answered, the hair on her arms standing up.

"That's right. I thought you should know."

"Yeah, thanks," Kate answered. "Good to know. I'll bear that in mind. Anything else?"

"No, that's it, the DCI is happy for you to enter the property based on what Stacy Lee said. Good hunting."

Thanking her, Kate ended the call, feeling a shiver of revulsion wash down her spine at the thought of Wilson knowing where she lived. Then she remembered the envelope that had been pushed under her door.

"Oh, crap. The envelope," she muttered.

"He knew who you were," Nathan said.

"Yeah, he did," she replied and wondered just how much he knew about her. Had he been watching her? Following her somehow? This just threw up even more questions. It could all be a coincidence of course, but somehow, part of her really wasn't sure she believed that.

Nathan pulled the car into a maze of commercial units that made up the North Way Industrial Estate just outside the city centre and paused at a map on the large sign just inside the gate. Kate craned her neck to get a better look.

"Got it," Nathan said, and set off, threading his way through the units and the parked cars outside of them. It soon became clear they were heading towards the back of the site, and moments later they turned up a spur that ended in a dead end, with a unit on their right. On their left, beyond a tall metal fence with spikes on top, was a small stretch of wasteland, with houses beyond.

Nathan turned the car around, and used it to block the exit out should Wilson get past them. He could still run past it, but he'd have trouble driving out of here.

There was only one car parked outside this unit, and Kate recognised it as one of the vehicles that had been at the Hollins' house when they had visited him the first time.

"Looks like he's here," Kate said, peering at the windows of the unit that were covered in metal grating. The building looked like it could do with some TLC and a fresh coat of paint.

"Maybe," Nathan answered her, his voice flat as he turned the engine off.

"Should we head inside?" Kate asked, those all too familiar butterflies flitting about her stomach at the thought of entering this creepy-looking building that likely housed a brutal killer. "Or maybe we should call in backup?"

"Both," Nathan answered, with a note of determination in his voice. "I want to get inside. If he's got Mark Summers in there, we can't waste any time."

"Of course," Kate answered, as Nathan grabbed the radio and spoke with dispatch, requesting backup at their location. The request was confirmed, and they informed Nathan it would be several minutes before they got to them.

Too long, Kate thought, as she remembered the photos of Mark that had been appearing for a few days now. Today had been the deadline that the killer had given, for whatever he had planned for Mark. Nathan was already getting out the car, so Kate joined him and moved to the boot where they pulled out their stab vests. With their protective clothing in place, Nathan made his way towards the front doors, his baton in hand. Kate followed, her eyes flicking from one window to another, wondering if someone might be watching them.

Grabbing the door handle, Nathan tried it. When it turned easily beneath his hand, he looked back at Kate. "Not too security conscious," he said.

"Or just very confident," Kate replied.

Nathan nodded and walked inside. Kate followed him into a reception area that was almost entirely empty of furniture or adornments of any kind. It looked disused but clean. Several doors led off from the space, including an open one to a side meeting room, that was also relatively empty.

"This isn't creepy at all," Kate commented sarcastically.

"I'll put in a complaint to the Union of Serial Killers for you, shall I?" Nathan asked.

"Would you? I'd appreciate that," Kate replied as she looked at the other doors. One of them was clearly marked as a restroom, the other said, 'Staff Only' on it.

"Let's check the bathroom first," Kate suggested.

Nathan nodded and followed her over. They burst inside, only to find an empty and clearly hardly used collection of stalls that made up the communal restroom.

Kate walked back out to where Nathan had waited by the door to watch the reception room. "Nothing," she said.

Nathan nodded. "Then we take door number two," he replied and led the way over.

He pulled it open and stepped through. "Hmm," he muttered, on seeing what was on the other side.

Kate followed only to find herself in a corridor leading deeper into the building. The hallways looked derelict, with dirty peeling walls, a messy floor, missing ceiling tiles, and trailing cables hanging from above. Dirt and dust were everywhere. It was in quite a state, Kate thought. Doors stretched along the corridor on either side and another at the end.

"Well, this just gets better and better," Kate said quietly. "Creepy corridor? Check!"

"Come on," Nathan said and started up the corridor. They reached the first door on their left, and Nathan pushed it open with his baton. It swung wide to reveal a disgusting bathroom that made Kate feel sick just looking at it. The smell didn't help either. Inside, Kate could see some obvious bloodstains on the floor and covering several of the basins in a dull red residue that had long since dried.

"Oh god," Kate said with a swallow.

"I think we found the right place," Nathan muttered.

"That's a big fat yes," Kate agreed as Nathan crept inside and checked the remains of the stalls along the left wall. Kate watched the corridor ahead and for a moment, felt sure she'd heard movement in the distance.

Kate hadn't done any firearms training, but it was during moments like this that the idea of carrying a gun felt like the most obvious thing in the world.

"Nothing in here, let's move on," Nathan said, stepping back into the corridor. "See anything?"

"No. Thought I heard something, but can't be sure," she whispered.

Nathan replied with a curt nod and focused his attention back up the hallway. As they moved, Kate noticed what looked like more bloodstains close to the next door ahead, on their right. It looked like someone, or something, had been dragged through here. They moved to the second door, and peeked through, to find a large, almost totally empty room in as bad a state of disrepair as the corridor. The only items in here were a hook on the end of a chain that hung from an exposed iron girder above the suspended ceiling, and a single chair that stood before it. The hook was stained red. The floor beneath it was also covered in the dried remains of blood.

"Homely, don't you think?" Kate muttered.

"No home is complete without a meat hook," Nathan answered as they both scanned the room. It was otherwise empty.

"I'll be sure to order one from Amazon," Kate replied as they moved back into the corridor. "Should work well in my studio flat."

The next room up was on their left again, with the door open, revealing a much smaller room with a desk and chair. A complicated computer workstation was set up on the desk, with a total of six monitors crowding around a single chair.

Picturesque photos of beautiful landscapes faded gently into one another on the screens, standing in stark contrast to the derelict nature of the rest of the room.

"What's he need this for?" Kate asked quietly.

Nathan narrowed his eyes. "I'm not sure," he replied as Kate moved into the room, checking the corners in case of ambush. Confident they were alone, she walked up to the desk, stepping over the cables that snaked away from the equipment to the wall, and gave the mouse a shake.

The screensaver flickered away to reveal the usual operating system on the bottom central monitor. Arrayed around it were feeds from what looked like security cameras. Kate didn't recognise most of them, but she quickly spotted one showing the outside of this unit, and their car parked outside.

"He might know we're here," Kate said, pointing to it.

Nathan looked and nodded. "Look here," he said and gestured to another feed. Kate peered at it, and it took a moment for her to recognise it.

"Shit, that's Jordan's office. He's been watching him with secret cameras?"

"I'll be willing to bet he's seen Jordan and Naomi in there, during their late night meetings."

"It's how he knew Jordan was at the office alone the other night."

Kate looked at the feeds with greater interest and quickly spotted one that showed the outside of Naomi's apartment block. She showed it to Nathan before she spotted one that made her blood run cold.

"Oh, shit," she said, as the bottom fell out of her stomach. She felt utterly sick as she stared at one of the feeds and the room she knew all too well.

"What?" Nathan asked.

Kate pointed at the image. "That, is the inside of my apartment."

"He's been watching you," Nathan said, stating the obvious.

"Yeah," Kate replied, wondering what he might have seen over the last few weeks. From the angle of the image, she felt sure the camera was hidden in a vent that she knew was on that wall.

"Nice décor, by the way," Nathan said.

Kate gave him a look. "Piss off."

She heard a thud come from another room and spun to look at the door behind them. Nathan did the same.

"This isn't over yet," he muttered and approached the door back out into the corridor. The hall was empty, and they continued up it, another room opening up on their left. It was similar to the one with the meat hook but was instead furnished with a single, soiled bed. The ancient mattress was covered in dark red, brown, and yellow stains, while sturdy leather straps hung from the metal bed frame. A single chair sat beside it, with a small, empty table beside that.

There were more bloodstains on the floor beside the bed. These fresher splatters of blood led away from it to the door they stood in, and along the corridor to the door at the end of the hallway. Some of the small pools of blood looked like a wheel of something had been pushed through them, leaving long tracks along the floor showing the progress of a wheelchair, or something on casters.

"This is going to give me nightmares for weeks," Kate muttered as they scanned the rest of the room, but found nothing.

"Only weeks? Wow, lucky you."

"Come on, he's in here somewhere," Kate said, and they both stepped back out into the corridor, following the fresh bloodstains. Two more doors lay ahead of them. One on their right, and the final one at the end of the hall.

The right-hand door led to an empty room with little of note inside, but the final door stood closed. Nathan stepped up to it and carefully tried the handle, but the door wouldn't move. It was locked.

"Crap," he whispered and stepped back. "Let's do this the hard way."

Nathan kicked the door, slamming his foot against it close to where Kate assumed the lock would be. The derelict nature of the building worked in their favour, and the door slammed open as wood splintered from the broken frame.

Nathan rushed inside, and Kate followed.

The room beyond was another big one, and in the middle of it was what looked like a tree, made from hundreds of dead branches and sticks, lashed together to form a large tree trunk.

Brown, dead leaves covered the floor, a few of them soaking up the blood that had been dripped on them. Strung up onto the tree, the remains of Mark Summers hung from the strange creation, his hands out wide in a pose that mimicked Christ on the cross. Mark's body had been flayed open, revealing his ribcage and the organs beneath it. Intestines hung like wet ropes from his stomach to the floor where they piled in the pool of blood beneath him. In front of him, a man kneeled on the floor, topless, facing the tree and the corpse, a dagger in one hand, his arms spread wide. Nearby, a bloody gurney stood discarded, no longer of use.

Nathan extended his baton with a flick of his wrist. Kate did the same.

"Wilson?" Nathan yelled.

The man laughed.

"Gary Wilson Hollins?"

"Aaah," the man said, his laugh stopping as he stood up, and turned to look at them. "You figured it out then?"

It was Wilson, Kate thought, recognising him. He was covered in blood, with strange symbols finger painted on his body drawn in the sticky red plasma. He had a wild expression on his face, but she recognised him none the less.

"Wilson Hollins, you're under arrest..."

"Shut up, you pitiful little creature. You can't get to me now. You're too late. The ritual is complete, and I am so much more now. I've seen so much. There is nothing you can do to me because I have been set free."

"You're under arrest," Nathan continued, "on suspicion of murdering Jordan Donaldson, Naomi Sawyer, and Mark Summers. You do not have to say anything," he continued, making his way through the wording for the Police Caution, while Wilson continued to rant about how he'd somehow ascended.

"You poor, idiot officers of the so-called law," Wilson said. "You have no idea of the truth. You have no idea what we know and how much we control. This is but the beginning. We will rise again; I can assure you of that. In fact, it has already begun."

"What are you talking about?" Kate replied, confused by his ramblings.

Wilson looked over at her, his chest glistening in the diffused light from the dirty windows.

"Kate. Beautiful Kate. How naive you are. It's been a pleasure watching you, you know. To see you learn what Nathan already suspects."

"Tell me what you know," Nathan barked at him.

Wilson looked back at Nathan and smiled. "Why should I? After all, we all have our secrets to keep, don't we?" he said, with a knowing look back at Kate.

Kate swallowed.

She did not like the look he just gave her and wondered what he might be referring to. Ireland maybe?

Nathan stepped closer, holding his baton threateningly. "Get on your knees and put your hands behind your head, interlocking your fingers."

Wilson looked back at Nathan with a smug grin. "Make me."

Nathan stepped closer to Wilson, his baton ready.

"Careful," Kate said.

"Listen to your partner," Wilson commented. "She knows what she's talking about."

Nathan lunged, probably hoping to catch him mid-speech when he was less ready for him, but Wilson moved quickly and stepped in closer. He grabbed Nathan's arm before the baton could strike him. Wilson twisted Nathan's wrist and thrust his other hand forwards. The hand with the knife.

Kate rushed forward, swinging her own baton and hitting Wilson on the forearm. He yelled in pain and withdrew from Nathan, who fell back.

"You bitch. You fucking bitch. You could have broken my arm."

"You mean I didn't? Damn, mind if I try again?"

"You think you're so clever, with your radios and sticks. But you're nothing. Do you hear me? Nothing! You have no idea what's out there. No idea at all."

"Do you ever talk sense?" Kate asked, keen to keep him talking as she stood over Nathan, protecting him, hoping that the Armed Response Team would hurry up. She needed backup.

"But I guess you might know something. Just a little something."

"I know all sorts of things," Kate replied defiantly.

"What about, Ireland?"

"What?" Kate asked, suddenly alert.

Wilson smiled, but Kate saw nothing humorous there. "Aah, yes. Now that hit a nerve, didn't it?"

"What do you know about me and Ireland? Huh? What? What do you know?"

"Now, now, no need to get angry," he said, raising his empty hand in a calming manner, but it did nothing for her. She could almost feel her blood boiling up inside of her as he spoke. She wanted to know what, if anything, he knew about her past, and the death of her aunt.

"I'll show you angry. Tell me what you know!"

Wilson only smiled, and then rushed towards her, swinging his arm.

With her baton in both hands, she swung again as he rushed in at head height and caught him across the face.

Wilson yelled in pain as he dropped to the floor, the knife skittering away as Kate pulled her cuffs. She dropped one knee onto his back, not being too careful how heavily she landed on him and grabbed his left arm.

Within seconds she had both hands cuffed and was stepping away from the prone man. He turned his head and looked up at her.

"You bitch. This isn't the end, you know. No way."

"You'd better believe it. I want to know what you know for a start."

"Nothing. I know nothing. Just a lucky guess is all, stupid cow."

Kate frowned, unsure whether to believe him or not, but she knew she'd get to interview him, and maybe he'd spill something then.

"You're in for it, you know. You and your partner. You just wait..."

"Shut it, dickhead," she replied, having had enough of his crap. Climbing off him, she rushed over to Nathan. He held his hand to his hip where blood was seeping through this fingers. "How bad is it?"

"Ugh, I don't know. Have a look," he said.

Kate pulled his hand away and lifted his shirt to see the stab wound. It was bleeding quite badly, but it didn't look too deep.

From the other end of the building, she heard voices shouting, "Police."

"Down here," Kate called out, guiding them in. Seconds later, several officers ran into the room. They cursed as they saw the body of Mark hung up, but were soon assisting Kate and Nathan, and calling in an ambulance while Wilson continued to rave about utter nonsense.

CHAPTER 27

"You didn't have the decency to die on us, then?" DCI Dean said to Nathan. He was perched on the edge of his desk with a cheeky smile on his face as he spoke to them.

Kate looked sideways at Nathan, who smiled back. "Sorry boss, you're not getting rid of me that easily."

"It wasn't too serious then?" the DCI asked.

"About an inch deep. They sewed me up and sent me on my way. Desk duty for a few weeks, but I'm fine basically."

"Well, you're going to have your hands full processing everything from your arrest of Wilson anyway, so you've timed that quite nicely."

"Always looking to make your life easier, Skipper."

"Of course you are. So, he's confessed to it all then?"

Nathan nodded to Kate as he pressed his hand against where Kate knew the stab wound to be.

"That's right, sir. He couldn't very well deny killing Mark, and we found plenty of DNA linking him to both Jordan and Naomi's deaths, including video footage of him killing Naomi in her apartment from the hidden camera he had installed in her room. We also found footage of him kidnapping Jordan."

She'd spent hours talking to him, but apart from the facts, it was difficult to get him to elaborate on anything at all. His lawyer was one of the best in London, and he'd clearly been schooled on what to say, and what not to say.

"Creepy bastard," the DCI muttered.

"We're uninstalling the other cameras he had placed in his other properties, including the one in my apartment," Kate added.

DCI Dean nodded. "Very good. Looks like we've got him bang-to-rights then."

"It appears that way, sir."

"What about all the occult stuff? What was that all about?"

"We're not sure, to tell you the truth. He's not really telling us much. That lawyer of his is causing us all kinds of trouble."

"How on earth did Wilson Hollins get Clement Alexander Parish as his lawyer? Even if he could afford him, why would he defend someone like Wilson?"

"I've no idea sir, but he's a nightmare to deal with."

"Alright, well, keep at it. Maybe he'll slip up."

"Will do, sir. Also, FYI, Mark's family has been informed of his death, as well."

"Good, thanks. Well done, both of you. This was some impressive work."

"I couldn't have done it without Kate," Nathan said.

Kate blushed at the compliment. It was a little unexpected, but she took it anyway.

"I can see that. Well, thank you very much, you've got plenty to do though, so let's crack on."

"Sir," Nathan replied, and hobbled towards the door. Kate opened it for him and let him start to make his way through.

"Kate," DCI Dean called to her.

"Sir?" she answered.

"A word please, on your own," he said.

"Of course," she answered, swapping a brief glance with Nathan, who smiled at her, his expression suggesting that he knew what this was about, and was resigned to it.

Kate closed the door behind Nathan and turned to face the DCI, who gestured to one of the chairs as he moved around the desk and sat behind it.

"Thank you, sir," Kate said taking the offered seat. "What can I do for you?"

"How have you found your first week here? It's been an eventful few days for you."

"It has, sir. Yes. But it's been good, thank you."

"And Nathan?"

"What about him, sir?" Kate asked, slightly confused.

"Did you work well with him?"

She shrugged. "I guess."

"Okay. Well, as I said when you joined us, your posting with Nathan was a temporary one and based on your performance over the past week, I think we can find you a more permanent partner. Someone less focused on conspiracy, shall we say?"

"Um, sir. May I speak freely, please?"

"Of course."

"With all due respect, sir, I would actually prefer to stay Nathan's partner. If that's okay with you?"

The DCI's eyebrows raised. "Are you sure?"

Kate smiled. "Quite sure, sir. I feel that we worked well together and that we complement each other's skill sets. So, if it's all the same, I'd prefer to stay put. If that's okay with DS Halliwell of course."

"Hmm," he replied, looking a little surprised and confused, but then seemed to accept her judgement. "As you wish. Providing Nathan is alright with this, then I am too."

Kate smiled. "Thank you, sir."

Kate returned to her desk to find Nathan sitting back, relaxing in his seat. He looked a little stiff and tense due to the wound. Kate thought he'd returned to work far too soon, but Nathan was having none of it.

"It's been good working with you, Kate," Nathan said, opening one eye as she neared their desks.

"I'm glad. And it's a good thing too, because you're going to be stuck with me for a while longer yet."

Nathan opened the other eye as well. "What do you mean? You'll be moving on to another partner, right?"

Kate smiled. "Nope. I refused the offer. I'm happy to continue as your partner."

"Really?" Nathan asked.

"Don't sound so surprised," Kate admonished him.

"Oh, okay, sure," he replied, a smile growing on his face. "Sounds good."

"Glad you're happy about it."

"I am. That's good news. I was getting a little frustrated by the constant turnover of partners, to be honest."

Kate smiled. "Well, no more. You're stuck with me. How about I bring in some Fig Rolls to celebrate?"

Nathan blinked. "DCI Dean? I'd like to object to this decision," he called out.

"Alright, alright, I'll bring some nobs in for you to guzzle."

Nathan smiled. "Hobnobs, I'll have you know!"

Kate winked and clicked her tongue at the same time. "Gotcha."

Nathan nodded with satisfaction, and Kate smiled to herself as she returned to her desk and started to wade through the paperwork that needed filling out and completing.

As she worked, her mind wandered, and she thought about the surveillance that Wilson had her under, and how much planning something like that would take, and something about it just didn't sit well with her.

"You know, it's all a little too convenient for my liking, you know? Me ending up in the flat that just so happens to be bugged by the very first person I investigate for the Murder Team. It's all a bit suspect."

Nathan turned to her and nodded. "Yeah, it is. I've been thinking the same thing. Something like that takes time and planning. It's not something you can do randomly or set up in a matter of days. But then, that would suggest they knew what was going to happen. It would suggest some kind of conspiracy."

Kate nodded. "You might be right…"

CHAPTER 28

Two men sat in a dimly lit room, on brown leather, wing-back chairs, facing each other and enjoying a glass of brandy.

"Did he succeed?" asked the first.

"We'll find out soon enough. We have our man going in as his solicitor," the second answered.

"Hmm. Wilson always was a bit of a wild card."

"He got a little too public, a little too quickly,"

"Perhaps. But if we're going to succeed, some subtlety will need to be sacrificed. Do you have a plan in place in case he talks?"

"Of course. He'll be found having committed 'suicide', which given the nature and severity of his crimes, shouldn't be much of a stretch. We'll be suggesting he pleads insanity anyway."

"That's a long shot."

"Worth trying."

"I guess. What about those detectives? Mr Halliwell has come close to us before. Looks like he's got a more permanent partner now."

"It does. We've been looking into them a little bit, but we're getting some resistance."

"Resistance?"

"I think, perhaps, our enemies might be aware of them."

"That's not good. The Herald will not be pleased."

The second man shrugged. "I'm not worried. We'll deal with them if we have to."

"I see. Very good. What about the hunt for the book? Any progress?"

"Some. Time will tell."

"Excellent," the second man replied, and raised his glass. "May the Grey Queen find us worthy."

The first man nodded, clinked his glass against the other one, and took a sip of his drink, savouring the flavour. Exciting times were coming, that was for sure.

CHAPTER 29

Kate walked up to the building that housed her small apartment. It looked like a large house and had probably been just that, once upon a time. But it had long since been divided up into small apartments, varying from the larger ones with more rooms on the ground floor, to the four studio apartments on the top floor, one of which was hers.

Walking in through the communal front door, she found several letters on the side waiting for her, placed there by whomever had been first to sort through them.

She picked them up and made her way upstairs into her flat, closing the door behind her.

Her place consisted of two rooms, the bathroom and the living space. The latter had a small kitchenette, and served as both her living room and bedroom as well.

She threw the letters on the countertop and hung her coat on the back of the front door, but stopped partway through the action. Had she seen what she thought she had?

Looking back at the countertop, one of the letters was handwritten and postmarked from Ireland.

Knowing what this letter was, her stomach dropped, and she felt slightly nauseated at the thought of it. Even so, a fascination with it fell over her, and she found herself reaching out for it and lifting it from the countertop.

Her name and address were written in the same handwriting she had come to know so well, and knew would be a match for all the other letters she'd received over the past ten years since her aunt's murder.

Letters that were from Fiona's murderer.

For a moment, as often happened, she considered throwing it in the bin, or burning it, but then her curiosity got the better of her, and she ripped it open. She wanted to know what the bastard was going to say to her this time.

Kate.

Congratulations. You've finally captured your first killer. Well done. How did it feel? Was it good? Did you get a thrill? A rush, when you finally had him in those cuffs?

I know what that's like. I know the thrill of the hunt all too well. But you know that, don't you?

Was the feeling as intense as the one you had when you confronted Duane back in Ireland?

I'm guessing it was probably not quite the same, was it? Did you hurt this killer as much as you hurt Duane? Or does putting someone behind bars, not quite match up to putting someone on life support?

Maybe I will get to ask you sometime.

Would you like that? Would you like to meet me... again...?

I could, perhaps, come to Surrey and show you how a real killer operates. How about that? Really give you something to chase.

Maybe that would give you that thrill again.

Or, how about I inform DS Halliwell about what you did in Ireland? That might be fun too.

What do you say?

I'll be watching...

Rage had slowly boiled up inside her as she'd read the letter, and she hated that she couldn't tell anyone about them. Not without potentially incriminating herself.

But that had been self-defence. Duane had attacked her when she'd confronted him and blamed him for the murder of her aunt. She hadn't attacked him. Hell, she hadn't even meant to hurt him.

She wondered if the Irish Garda would see it that way though. It was so long ago now that the details sometimes got a little confused in her mind.

Frustrated, she screwed up the letter and threw it across the room, knowing that she'd find it later, flatten it out, and put it in the folder with all the others she'd received over the years.

With a sigh, she sat on her bed and buried her head in her hands as she tried to calm down. Eventually, she looked up and stared at the screwed up paper ball on the floor.

"I'll get you, you little shit. One day, I will get you, I promise you that."

Author Note

Thank you so much for reading this, my first Novel. It has been a joy to finally get this done, and I really hope you liked it.

Of course, this isn't the end of Kate and Nathan's adventures, and I have plans for many more books in this series.

I've always enjoyed thrillers and thought about the idea of writing one. I even wrote a Murder Mystery interactive play once, but it wasn't until I recently watched the first series of True Detective, that the idea of finally trying to write a thriller took hold.

This series is very much inspired by that series and films like Seven, and I'm looking forward to fleshing out this world and slowly revealing more of it to you.

Book 2 is next, and I will be getting on with that very soon. By the time you read this, it will likely already be underway.

Thanks again for reading this book. If you enjoyed it, I'd very much appreciate a review on Amazon.

Word of mouth is an author's best friend and much appreciated.

Remember though, no spoilers in the review. :-)

In the meantime, you can always catch up with me on my Facebook page, here; www.facebook.com/ALFraineAuthor

You can also join my mailing list and download the free prequel by clicking here: https://dl.bookfunnel.com/dbeuremmfr

See you in book 2.
A L Fraine.Surrey, UK.
www.alfraineauthor.co.uk

Book List

DC O'Connell British Crime Thrillers
First Hand – Prequel
The Upper Hand – Book 1
Idle Hands – Book 2
Out of Hand – Book 3

Printed in Great Britain
by Amazon